The Tale of
KAKAMUCHU

Corvidae Publishing

Los Angeles, California

The Tale of Kakamuchu

Copyright © 2012 by Marjan Massoudian

Printed in the United States of America

First Edition, 2012

www.kakamuchu.com

Publisher's Cataloging-in-Publication

Massoudian, Marjan.

   The tale of Kakamuchu / Marjan Massoudian. — 1sted.
   p. cm.

   SUMMARY: Two friends secretly devise a plan to resist
   a tyrannical leader who bans laughter on their planet.

   Audience: Ages 8-10.

   LCCN 2012906739

   ISBN 978-0-615-62981-0

   1. Laughter — Juvenile fiction. 2. Liberty — Juvenile fiction.
   [1. Laughter — Fiction. 2. Freedom — Fiction.
   3. Fantasy.] I. Title.

PZ7.M423862Tal 2012   [Fic]
                  QBI12-600097

                        Book Design by Pastilla Studio
                  Cover Illustrations by Chia-Yi Lin

For Leili, Reiv and Raz

TABLE OF CONTENTS

PROLOGUE

"Oh no, Henrite! Another note from school about an incomplete assignment? This is the second one this week!"

"Sorry, Mom!" Henrite was about to put on his gaming helmet to start playing. He was allowed to play for half an hour before doing his homework. On his planet, Kaka-La, gaming helmets attached to brain waves and actually took a player inside a game. Henrite loved fantasy games where he got to create worlds the most. There were no war games on Kaka-La, because there had never been any kind of war in their history. There were mean Royal Guards, but, all together, they were tolerable.

"Sweetie, your teachers are being really understanding given the circumstances."

"I know, Mom. Could I please play my game first? My friends are already hooked in."

"Okay. Have some fun with your friends. But then do your homework. You are not going to leave your teachers any choice but to keep you after school. As if you don't already spend enough time there!"

"You're the best, Mom!"

Henrite's mom turned back to checking messages on her tablet and Henrite put on his helmet.

Shelshala, Henrite's best friend, was already in the game, as were a few of his other friends. He was at level 55, only a level behind Shelshala! Kenakada was already at level 61, but he was mad good at games. No one had ever caught up with him in any game. But, there was a real chance Henrite might move ahead of Shelshala or at least tie her level. She would freak out if he moved ahead of her! She was crazy competitive, even though she always insisted she was not.

His next mission was an obstacle course through an enchanted forest. Once he nailed it, he would have enough points to add a racetrack to his city. The Kakamuchu Speed Relay Race at his school was coming up and he was totally psyched that he and Shelshala had both made the team this year. He should probably add another energy plant to his city instead so there wouldn't be any more blackouts, but he didn't care. He wanted a racetrack. He'd deal with the blackouts later.

Henrite was completely absorbed in avoiding a fairy, which was trying to catch a ride on his back to slow him down, when his helmet shut off. Dad was home. Henrite's thirty minutes were up and his dad had remotely switched off his game.

Henrite took off his helmet. "Ah, Dad. I'm almost on level 56! Could I have five more minutes?"

"Hi son and no. Homework."

"Drats!" Henrite headed towards the ramp to his room. "It's not my fault we have to stay in school until the sun goes down. There's no time for fun. This planet sucks!"

Little did Henrite know that things were about to get a lot more unpleasant.

1

THE PLANET KAKA-LA

It was a day like any other day on Planet Kaka-La.

Kids got ready for school, parents for work and farmers prepared for the morning markets.

The inhabitants of Kaka-La, called Kakalilians, looked very different from humans on Earth.

For one thing, they had wheels that grew out of their feet. Under each big toe was a button they used to control speed. Each push of the button on their right foot made them go faster and a push on the button on their left foot slowed them down.

For everyday needs within the city, they used the slower speeds. If they made a trip outside the city, such as to the wilderness for a picnic, they would use higher speeds. It took a while to learn how to use the different speeds. Children who were learning how to 'wheel' often crashed into things and people until they got the hang of changing gears.

As different looking as the Kakalilians were to humans, in many ways they were just like us.

They loved their families and friends and cared about the wellbeing of their planet. They recycled, reused and replanted and always had their homes open for visitors with whom they shared the native drink: Laka-kaka-lali (Kakalilian lemonade).

All in all, Kaka-La was a great place to live because of its people. But there was one BIG exception...

Their ruler, Kakamuchu, was as mean as the day is long.

He woke up mean.

Ate breakfast mean.

Was mean to the servants who helped him change into his royal clothes.

Used the morning to plan mean things to do to the people of Kaka-La.

Wouldn't eat lunch, so he would become even grumpier.

Spent his afternoons alone in his laboratory working on mean experiments.

Then, ate dinner mean, went to sleep mean and dreamed of mean things...

Only to wake up mean again to start another day.

On THIS soon-to-be-dreadful day, no one had any idea how mean Kakamuchu was going to be.

2

THE MOST DREADED DAY

Usually Kakamuchu just stayed in his castle and let his staff do everything for him. But on THIS day, he decided to leave his castle atop Mount KalaKala to visit Kakamuchuville.

He normally visited the capital city only once a year for the Kakamuchu-Is-the-Best-Leader-in-the-Galaxy Festival. The organizers of the festival worked with the castle staff for weeks to make sure the festival did not include anything that might make Kakamuchu angrier than he was naturally.

For some reason—who knows why?—On THIS soon-to-be-terrible day, he decided to arrive at the city unannounced.

He believed it was undignified to wheel in public, so a royal vehicle called a Kaka-luto had been made especially for his use.

On THIS day, as Kakamuchu sat on cushioned velvet seats in his Kaka-luto and moved through the city, he was looking out the window at the morning activities. He did not plan on stopping anywhere, as he thought he was too important to talk with 'regular' Kakalilians.

When he passed through the city center, where preparations were being made for the daily outdoor market, he heard a sound he did not recall hearing before, a sound that immediately made his purple blood boil and his ears turn green. He did not know why the sound made him so angry, even more angry than usual.

He just did not like it. It sounded...too happy. "What could it be?" he thought. And then, he had a flash of memory from when he was a very young child.

It was the sound of laughter.

3

KAKAMUCHU
MUST BE KIDDING!

On THIS soon-to-be-terrible day, Little Balabalka walked around the market, investigating the hustle and bustle. His dad was not feeling well, so his mom, a farmer, had brought him to the market with her. She was readying their stall by piling turpanays on a table. (A turpanay is a Kakalilian vegetable infused with the flavor of cotton candy so kids will enjoy eating it.)

The other farmers and their helpers stopped their work to play with him or give him something sweet to eat. One farmer tickled him under his arm and Balabalka laughed right out loud.

It was exactly at this moment that Kakamuchu's Kaka-luto passed by. The farmer immediately stopped tickling the young boy and turned to bow. Unaware, Little Balabalka continued to laugh.

Upon hearing the laughter, Kakamuchu sat right up and yelled at his driver, "You incompetent irritant. Why did you bring me here? Take me back to the castle right away!"

As soon as he entered the castle, he yelled for the Prime Minister who came wheeling at high speed.

Breathless, the Prime Minister said, "Yes, Your Mega

Uber Majesty. How may I be of service?"

"Right this moment, write a decree that laughter is no longer permitted in Kaka-La. Send it throughout the land!" commanded Kakamuchu.

The Prime Minister was a very patient man who always did whatever his ruler asked. He was accustomed to hearing ridiculous decrees. But, in this case, he could not help but protest.

"Kind Mega Uber Majesty, laughter is spontaneous. It cannot be prohibited."

The poor Prime Minister's attempt to stop the nonsensical decree only made Kakamuchu angrier.

"You dare to question my will! Not only is laughter banned throughout the land, laughter will be punished with the Vanisher! As of tomorrow when I awaken, Kaka-La is to be a laugh-less land! Go, you nincompoop and do as I say! Do not ever question my authority again. I am Divine Anointed Leader Supreme of Kaka-La and will have you vanished too, if you disobey me!"

The poor downtrodden Prime Minister felt miserable. If only he had not protested, maybe laughter would have been punished only with a ticket. But, now, look what he had done. The Vanisher!

4

HENRITE AND SHELSHALA

Also at the market on that soon-to-be-dreaded day were Henrite and Shelshala. Shelshala's mom had asked her to go to the market to get a few things and Henrite had tagged along.

As much as their parents encouraged them not to have ill feelings toward Kakamuchu, they could not help but think that he really sucked. His behavior at the market was just one more example of how much he sucked. They could not remember a time when their ruler had been anything but mean. The little kid hadn't done anything wrong! What was Kakamuchu's problem? Why did he have to make everyone so nervous?

Henrite got so mad he picked up a piece of fruit from atop one of the carts and aimed it at Kakamuchu's Kaka-luto as it headed back toward the castle.

Shelshala grabbed his arm mid air. "Are you nuts? There are guards everywhere!"

Henrite didn't resist as she pushed down on his arm. "Darn it! Okay! You can let go of my arm. I won't do anything stupid."

"Stupid doesn't even begin to cover it!" Shelshala glared at him and put the piece of fruit back on the cart.

"Whatever. Let's just hurry up, buy your mom's stuff, and go home."

Henrite and Shelshala had been friends since they were babies. Their houses were right next to each other and their parents had been friends for as long as they could remember.

Henrite's mom was a sculptor and his dad was an astronomer who worked in one of Kaka-La's energy plants where starlight was converted to energy. The scientists of the energy plant regularly went to space, collected star-energy and brought it back to Kaka-La.

Once, Henrite and Shelshala got to go up with his dad into space. It was so cool! The ship they had travelled in was coated with a special heat resistant material, because even the smaller stars they visited could reach temperatures of 3000 degrees Celsius (about 5400 degrees Fahrenheit). They also had to wear special glasses to protect their eyes from the spectacular reddish light radiating from a star. Without them, they would have been blinded in less than a second.

After a special vacuum had sucked up energy from a few stars and stored it in tanks for transport back to Kaka-La, his dad had taken them for a space tour, telling them about the planets in their galaxy and the many different kinds of light rays that exist in the universe. He showed them the glowing band of their spiral galaxy that had been re-named Kakamuchu's Way when Kakamuchu came to power. It included a glittering mass of stars that looked like an eyeball. Everything had been so amazing! They had a great time in space, but couldn't travel too far away from Kaka-La or the Royal Guards would be waiting to interrogate Henrite's dad when they got back. Scientists and engineers were not allowed to go beyond a certain point in the galaxy without getting permission ahead of time.

Shelshala's mom was an inventor and her dad an electrical engineer. Her mom's lab took up almost half of their home. The kids loved to spend time there. Some of her inventions, such as the Grubster, were used across Kaka-La.

The Grubster was a kitchen tool that could cook a hot breakfast while everyone was asleep. Before going to bed, the user put ingredients for Kakalilian style eggs and bacon, or pancakes in the Grubster, set the timer for the next day's breakfast and, voila! When everyone woke up, breakfast was ready.

There were also inventions she had made for fun, like the Poop-Out Companion. Each Poop-Out Companion was programmed to recognize the scent of its own ponggy (a Kakalilian dog), follow it on walks and clean up after it. In the beginning, the ponggies were terrified when their Poop-Out Companion followed them and would run inside and hide. But with a little training, they got used to it.

Henrite and Shelshala's parents always encouraged them to think for themselves and learn about everything. "If you love learning, you never run out of things to love," Henrite's mom always said when he complained about schoolwork.

"Sure thing, mom," Henrite would say whenever his mom tried to convince him that learning was a good thing, just to make her happy. But, as far he was concerned, if he could play games with his friends all day and avoid going to school altogether, life would be perfect. Well, almost perfect. If Kakamuchu disappeared, THEN it would be totally perfect!

5

THE STORY OF KAKAMUCHU
AND THE VANISHER

You may be wondering why Kakamuchu was so mean.
Henrite and Shelshala had heard the story a number of
times. Their parents thought that if they understood why
he was so mean, maybe they wouldn't think he was so bad.
Yeah, right!

Kakamuchu's mother had died when he was a toddler
and his father's heart had broken and turned to stone.
Before her death, the castle had been full of laughter, music,
singing and fun. All its inhabitants dressed in colorful
clothes and sparkling crystals from the mountains (all
the mountains in Kaka-La are made of different colored
crystals).

After the Supreme Leader's heart turned to stone, all the
fun Kakalilians were banished from the castle. Those who
remained shuffled through its halls and rooms with their
heads down, staring at their toes.

The only activity Prince Kakamuchu IV was permitted
was studying. No friends, no games, no outdoor play, only
studying day and night to prepare for one day becoming the
Supreme Leader.

The people of Kaka-La felt very sorry for their leader

when he lost his wife and tried hard to be kind to him. But he refused to see anyone. He remained locked up in the castle and left the Kakalilians to live their lives without interference.

They also felt very sorry for little Kakamuchu. But after a while they forgot about him, because he never left the castle or had his picture in the newspapers or magazines. It was only after his father died and Kakamuchu IV became the Supreme Ruler that they learned what an unhappy creature he had become.

As a child, he had used all the science he learned for inventions that do mean things. The only time he smiled and shouted with pleasure "Kakamuchu Rules!" was when he was in his lab and one of his inventions became a success. His poor nannies — and then, as he grew older, his tutors — almost always were the test subjects for his inventions. After he learned about anatomy, he created a cream to make hair fall out. He made his nanny spread it all over her head and in a matter of minutes she was bald.

He made his tutor drink a potion that made the poor man burp all day. He burped so much he couldn't eat and had to go to the hospital and have food injected directly into his stomach for days until the doctors figured out how to stop his burping.

When Kakamuchu learned about the electromagnetic spectrum, including all the different kinds of light waves in the universe like ultraviolet and gamma rays, his mind immediately turned to what evil use he could make of his newfound knowledge. He came up with the idea of the "Vanisher", a high-powered ray gun that released a beam able to shatter a target into a million matter particles that vanished into thin air. At first, his goal had been to vanish objects around the castle so everyone would be confused and constantly looking for things.

But one day, as he hid behind a curtain intending to shoot the lesson plan calendar on his tutor's desk, he accidently shot his tutor instead. To Kakamuchu's delight, his tutor vanished. Kakamuchu jumped with joy when he saw that the Vanisher worked on living as well as non-living matter. At the same time, he knew that if anybody else disappeared, the Vanisher would be taken away from him. So, he hid it in a safe place, knowing that one day, when he became the supreme ruler of Kaka-La, he would use the Vanisher to make everyone obey him.

Eight years later, when he became Mega Uber Ruler of the land, he had put his plan into action.

6

THE ROYAL GUARDS

When he became Supreme Leader, Kakamuchu brought
to Kaka-La a band of bandits from a neighboring planet,
Doofusturn, to become his elite guard. Each of them was
equipped with the Vanisher gun he had invented years
before. Kakamuchu made slight tweaks to the gun's
design so that the pieces of the Vanished would come
back together somewhere in the galaxy only he knew
the location of. He thought this made him a very kind ruler.
After all, he could have just continued vanishing targets
into thin air without putting the pieces of their bodies
back together again!

The guards were about three times taller and two times
wider than an average Kakalilian adult, but their heads
were very small in comparison. They were not bright and
had very bad tempers. Henrite's dad joked that they were
always losing their tempers because thinking put too much
pressure on their tiny brains.

Kakamuchu liked that his guards did not think much
and obeyed him without question. But, after bringing them
to Kaka-La, he soon realized that their uncontrollable
tempers were a problem. They would shoot the Vanisher at
anything when they were angry, even at their own feet. So
Kakamuchu invented a range regulator, which he implanted

in each guard's arm. Whenever a guard's blood pressure rose beyond a certain level, the regulator immediately injected medicine into the guard's arm to bring it down.

It was always fun to watch a guard when he got a dose of medicine from the regulator. For some reason, right before a guard's blood pressure returned to normal, he would bop himself in the face. Because of this reaction to the medicine, most of the guards always walked around with a black eye, bruised cheek, or busted nose. But, they never lost their tempers and that was all Kakamuchu cared about.

So guards used the Vanishers to enforce Kakamuchu's supreme decrees. Disobedient Kakalilians would — poof! — vanish into thin air. They also gave out public disturbance tickets for so called 'less severe' violations, which basically meant for any reason they felt like.

The first time Shelshala and Henrite had seen a guard getting a dose of medicine, they couldn't help laughing hysterically. That is until another guard passed by and gave them (and a few other laughers) Unacceptable Unruly Behavior in Public! tickets.

Adults who received three or more Unacceptable Unruly Behavior in Public tickets in a year would have to attend a Be a Good Citizen camp for a week. While there, complete silence was required while eating only bread and water and watching a movie about how great Kakamuchu's decrees were for the peace and prosperity of Kaka-La. The movie repeated for twelve hours a day for the whole week! Kids under 13 years of age were not sent to camp. Instead, they were given No-Fun Discipline for a week. Henrite had been given No-Fun Discipline when he was nine and never forgot how miserable it was to be cooped up in the house without friends or games to play with.

The Kakalilians got used to the guards always being around and, initially, even tried to make friends with them, but the guards weren't interested. The only activity they enjoyed was vanishing Kakalilians. The sound of guards yelling "Ootama!!" ('Ouch' in their language) as they hit themselves in the face was most often heard when months went by without them having a reason to shoot someone.

7

KAKAMUCHU'S
MEAN DECREES

You would think the Kakalilians would hate Kakamuchu for being such a tyrannical and mean leader. But this was not the case. While they could never understand how their leader could be so unkind, they were a gentle and compassionate people who did not like fighting.

So rather than hating Kakamuchu, they tried to do everything he asked in the hope that one day, he would learn not to be so angry. Perhaps happiness would finally enter his mind and heart.

When Kakamuchu demanded that they wear no colors but black and brown, they dyed all their colorful clothes accordingly. When he decreed that all children must go to school six days of the week from dawn to dusk without recess, the Kakalilians obeyed his wishes. When he banned candy from the markets, because he was in a particularly bad mood, the candy factories closed.

Yet, as mean as Kakamuchu was to his people, he could not suppress their natural tendency to be positive and happy.

Tailors and seamstresses embroidered funny pictures inside shirts, pants, skirts and dresses that made the Kakalilians laugh as they put on their clothes. Teachers made their classes extra fun, so the children would enjoy their lessons and not miss recess too much.

In response to the candy ban, mothers and fathers baked all kinds of sweet cakes and cookies. Children knew only to eat them at home so as not to upset their ruler.

The Kakalilians also did all they could to make their surroundings fun and colorful, especially their houses, which looked like eggs that have been cut flat near the bottom. Inside, ramps connected rooms and floors, so the occupants could wheel between them. Each house was painted to the owner's taste. Some were solid colors, with trim around the windows; others used sponge painting or painted designs or pictures on their houses. Kakalilians loved how the houses in their neighborhoods let everyone express their own personality.

So while Kakamuchu had intended to make his people sad, he'd instead made them more creative and innovative.

Of his numerous ridiculous decrees, one of the most difficult to obey was the ban on song and music. Almost every Kakalilian adult had at one time or another accidently hummed a tune they remembered from the past, but none, thank goodness, had ever been caught in the act. Most of the children had never heard music and parents preferred it that way so there would be no chance of accidental singing.

The Vanishers did generate unease across the land, but they were rarely used. The Kakalilians did their best not to break their leader's rules and, instead, find ways to replace forbidden fun with other types of fun.

So life was lived until the awful day when the No-Laughter decree changed everything.

8

THE NO-LAUGHTER DECREE

No laughter! How was that possible? Laughter is like breathing: you don't make it happen, it just does! For the first time, the resilient inhabitants of Kaka-La felt strong fear. How could they prevent laughter?

The timid royal advisors put their timidity aside and begged Kakamuchu to reconsider the decree, but he would not. Only the members of the Royal Guard were laughing inside as they eagerly awaited the opportunity to vanish all the Kakalilians. They were sick of the people's resilient spirits and positive attitudes.

Kakalilians organized town hall meetings to discuss the decree. Shelshala, Henrite and his little sister, Candicala, attended one of these meetings with their parents. People took turns expressing their fears and thoughts about how to deal with the decree. A number of Royal Guards also were standing around the hall monitoring the discussion.

"I am most concerned for the children. How are they going to remember not to laugh?" asked a lady holding her little daughter in her arms as she stood up to talk.

"Maybe we should consider homeschooling and not allow children to go outside without supervision," said another.

Everyone started talking among themselves about this idea.

"Wait, wait, dear friends. This cannot be a solution," said a tall male who got up from where he was sitting. "Laughter echoes and cannot be contained by walls!"

Henrite wasn't really paying attention to what the adults were saying. He just didn't get it. Why did the adults always try to keep Kakamuchu happy? If he were an adult, he would not just sit around and take it. He would come up with a plan.

He was daydreaming about stealing a Vanisher from one of the guards and wheeling up to Kakamuchu's castle, when the little girl in her mom's arms let out a big fart and started laughing. Her mom quickly sat down and covered her daughter's mouth, but it was too late. One of the guards had heard the laughter. From across the room, he shot the little girl with a Vanisher!

A pin drop could have been heard loud and clear as everyone stared in shock at the empty space where the little girl had been. A few seconds passed before her mother cried out in pain and others gathered around to comfort her. The meeting was adjourned and everyone quickly gathered up their children to rush home.

Shelshala burst into tears once she and Henrite were out of the building and wheeling home with their parents.

"Oh mom, that poor little girl! Her poor parents!"

Shelshala's mom had her arm wrapped tightly around Shelshala. "I know, love."

"Is it always going to be like this?" Shelshala asked as she gulped back her tears.

"Not if I can help it!" Henrite yelled.

"Henrite!" his dad said sharply.

Henrite's dad was a really calm person. He never yelled. Just from his tone, Henrite knew how upset he was.

Henrite's shoulders slumped as he lowered his head and stopped talking.

"Sorry, son. Now is not the time."

As they neared their homes, no one said a word.

One thing was crystal clear for Shelshala and Henrite: nothing would ever be the same again.

9

THE ERA OF SILENCE

So began the Era of Silence.

During the first week the No-Laughter decree was enforced, the Royal Guard vanished hundreds of Kakalilians. Over half of them were children. Shelshala and Henrite lost three of their classmates, two who had been vanished through an open bedroom window as they shared a funny story. Nowhere was safe from the guards.

Henrite's family had a very close call with his little sister. Since the No-Laughter decree had been implemented, Candicala was no longer allowed to go into the yard to play with Kalabbie, their ponggy. One day, she managed to squeeze herself out through the ponggy door in the kitchen and follow Kalabbie into the yard. As she ran after him, Kalabbie started chasing his tail and she burst out with laughter.

Henrite was in the kitchen when he heard the sound. He wheeled out the back door at lightning speed, grabbed his sister up off the ground and made a dash back into the house. Candicala was so startled she started screaming and punching him.

"Candi, be quiet! Please!"

Henrite felt as if his heart was beating a thousand times a minute. As he stood up against a wall with his sister wiggling in his arms, he heard the dreaded hum of a motokalin, the flying movers the guards used to patrol the streets. The sound came from their backyard.

After a few minutes, as Henrite struggled to keep his hand over Candicala's mouth, the hum became fainter as the guard moved away. Henrite relaxed and let Candicala slip to the floor. His arms were cramped from holding her so tightly. She kicked his shin and ran away from him. As a sharp pain shot up his leg where her front wheel had bitten into his skin, he gave a sigh of relief and promised himself that he would never give her a wedgie again!

With time, as more and more of their family members, friends and neighbors vanished, Kakalilian laughter came to a natural end. Life in the city became as dreary as life in the castle.

All of Kakamuchu's cabinet members and the Prime Minister, who had been loyal to him throughout his reign and had tolerated his decrees, abandoned their posts after their failed attempts to convince him to put an end to the horrible No-Laughter decree. Kakamuchu was going to have the guards vanish them all, but then decided it was not worth the effort. After all, they were the ones losing the privilege of serving him. In his egotistical mind, this was a punishment far worse than vanishing!

Only Kakamuchu and his personal Elite Guards remained in the castle. The guards took over all the palace duties. Every evening, just before Kakamuchu retired for the night, they would let him know the number of vanishings for the day.

He kept a running tally on his tablet. But no matter how high the number got, it did not give him any satisfaction. In fact, a few times, for a split second, he felt bad. But then, he quickly shook the feeling off and thought to himself: "It's not my fault that they choose not to obey my decree. After all, I have no trouble not laughing. If they were more like me, there would be no more Vanishings!"

10

THE SHRINE OF THE MISSING

As the number of the Vanished increased, the Kakalilians set up a shrine to remember the missing in the wilderness surrounding the city.

The dirt of Kaka-La was made of mineral rich gold dust that nurtured the trees and plants. When it rained the leaves fell from the trees to the ground. There they absorbed minerals from the gold dust and then floated back up onto the trees.

They fed on the ground minerals and never died, instead changing colors throughout the year: sparkling red when they were full of minerals, orange when losing minerals, and yellow when they had almost run out. It was quite an amazing sight to see all the sparkling leaves dancing in the sky as they flew back up onto the tree branches.

Kakalilians would go to the wilderness on their day off to have picnics and, if it hadn't rained in a long time, would also shake tree branches to help the yellow leaves fall. On these trips, they would also visit the Shrine of the Missing. They didn't have to worry too much about the Royal Guards being in the wilderness, because they hated nature and much preferred harassing people in the city.

The Shrine had started with a few Kakalilians hanging

pictures of their vanished loved ones on a cave wall. The cave was very large with a narrow entrance hidden from view behind a copse. As more and more Kakalilians were vanished, the pictures multiplied.

Soon, word of the cave spread across the city and a group of carpenters secretly carved beautiful benches with native russet wood for visitors to sit on. Electricians added motion sensor battery operated lanterns to the ceiling. A long table was built and placed in the center of the cave. Local artists engraved the names of each of the Vanished on it, using the names on the pictures hanging on the walls. As the number of the Vanished increased, a second table was added.

Visitors to the Shrine brought nuggets of crystal. Beside each carved name lay a glittering piece of crystal in memory of the lost. A few months after the No-Laughter decree, the crystals numbered in the thousands. When visitors were in the cave, the lights from the ceiling reflected off the crystals onto the walls, spreading a warm shimmering light on the images of the Vanished.

Shelshala and Henrite had both visited the Shrine with their families. It was sad and almost impossible to believe that all the faces on the wall had disappeared.

They wondered: had they survived? Did they have food and water?

The calm energy of the Shrine also created hopefulness. Sometimes, while sitting on a bench, Shelshala would imagine that all the Vanished had been transported to another beautiful planet like Kaka-La without a horrible leader. There they were busy building a new city, with farmers planting food, engineers building roads and architects designing houses, while scientists researched ways to get back in touch with loved ones on Kaka-La. She knew it was just a dream, but it made her hopeful — and hope made it possible to believe that, someday, everything would be all right again.

11

TRYING TO MAKE LIFE
A LITTLE LESS MISERABLE

Days continued without fun or laughter, everyday like the last, every night like the night before.

Shelshala and Henrite dreaded going to school. To make sure the kids would have no reason to laugh, their teachers had stopped making lessons fun. Instead, students spent all their time in the science lab, sifting through dirt to identify all the particles or watching mold grow. One time, when two kids playfully started throwing dirt at each other, their science teacher, Mrs. Jamalku, immediately took it away from them. She made them read a book about dirt and write a summary instead.

History lessons were even worse: all about other planets where environmental damage, war, or famine had destroyed all the inhabitants. So depressing!

All color paints, pencils and chalk had been removed from their art classes. Kids were allowed to use black and brownish colors and were told to draw subjects like 'A pitch dark night' or 'A rotten mozzlie' (a Kakalilian banana).

After school was no better. They were not allowed to play outside. At home, they could either read (boring books their parents read first to make sure nothing funny happened) or wheel up and down the ramps of the house for exercise.

To try to find some relief from the non-stop boredom, Henrite and Shelshala formed a secret club for their class. Most kids had hidden a few comic books on memory buttons before their parents erased all fun things from their tablets. Shelshala was responsible for keeping track of the sharing network and she created a spreadsheet with all the readers and available books. She asked Kenakada, one of their classmates who was really great with computers, to write software that would match available books with readers, based on what they had and had not read. It was a kind of virtual library.

Kenakada was the kind of guy who didn't say much but was really smart. He liked Shelshala a lot and would do pretty much anything she asked. But, she didn't know that, because he always played it real cool.

Every morning, using the school messaging network, kids who finished a book would send an in-class question to Shelshala or Henrite's tablet. They made it look like a question about one of their classes. Shelshala and Henrite would then enter the sender into the program Kenakada had created. The computer program matched all available books with requests for books. Once the program had made all the matches, Shelshala and Henrite answered the notes they had received from their classmates with a made-up response that included the name of the person to trade a book with.

So one kid might send a message to Henrite that said: What chapter are we supposed to read for our science project?

And Henrite would respond, I'm not sure. You might want to ask Pamalali. She's already started reading.

The kids would then exchange memory buttons sometime before school finished.

The club was working perfectly and spread across different classes at their school. But, like everything else on Kaka-La, the fun didn't last long. A kid named Andernala didn't hear his mom come into his room to bring him a snack. She caught him smiling as he was reading a comic book and sent an emergency message to all the parents about how he'd gotten it. That immediately put an end to the secret club.

And games, forget about that! All gaming helmets had been put in recycling bins and then picked up by city trucks. Parents weren't taking any chances that the kids might figure out a way to play games.

After months of just-shoot-me-and-get-it-over-with boredom, Shelshala and Henrite could no longer take it.

"I've had it! No games, no jokes, no candy and mind numbing boring classes! Why don't they just shot us and get it over with!" said Henrite one day as they headed home from school.

"I know! I wanted to scream in history class when she talked about every single battle that happened on Planet Indearus before it was destroyed by an asteroid. All right already, I get it! They were violent and couldn't stop killing each other! At least the asteroid finished off their miserable lives!"

Henrite didn't say anything. What Shelshala had been saying made him think of something.

A few seconds passed.

"Henrite?"

"Huh. Yeah. Sorry. I was thinking."

"What about?"

"The killing thing. It sure would be nice to get rid of the guards!"

"Henrite, that's a terrible thing to say!" Shelshala said as she quickly glanced around to see if any guards were nearby.

Henrite lowered his voice. "No, I don't mean kill them. Just get rid of 'em. On Indearus they fought over stupid things like land and energy, things they coulda shared. We're different. We should be looking for a way to get rid of the guards just so we can have normal lives."

"Henrite, sometimes you say the craziest things! Let's just talk about something else."

"Okay. How 'bout the race? That should at least be some fun! We're supposed to come up with the super charging strategy for our turbochargers."

Every year, all the city middle schools entered three teams each in the Kakamuchu Speed Relay Race. This was the first year Henrite and Shelshala were on a team for their school. The race was pretty dangerous, as each team was allowed to modify their wheels to go as fast as they could without becoming airborne for longer than five seconds at a time. There were always gnarly accidents, as one or more of the teams made their wheels faster than they could manage. The Royal Guards loved the race because of all the collisions.

The race was usually the highlight of the school year: the only real fun kids got to have.

"The race isn't for another three months or so. We're gonna need to do a ton of research on turbochargers," said Shelshala.

"You and the research! We should just send a message for the team that won last year and ask them what they did," said Henrite.

"First of all, that's cheating. And, do you think you're the only one who came up with that bright idea?"

"Oh yeah, good point."

"I'll talk with my mom and dad and see what they think we should do," said Shelshala.

"Okay, I'll also run it by my dad. I can't wait!!!! Finally, a little fun around this place!"

"Don't count on it." Shelshala jokingly imitated a decree announcement: "Decree number one million, one hundred thousand and thirty-three: Relay Racing Shall No Longer be Permitted Throughout Kaka-La. If you race, we will shoot!"

Henrite gave a quick smile, but then, slumped his shoulders and quietly said: "Who knows. Maybe he'll take that away for us too."

As much as they wanted to believe that would never happen, they both knew that as long as Kakamuchu was around, anything was possible.

12

WHAT IF?

"I've been thinking about what you said the other day," Shelshala said a few days later on their way home from school. The streets were pretty empty because it was later than when they usually wheeled home. Henrite had been assigned study hall to make sure he did his homework and Shelshala had hung around and done her homework as well so they could go home together.

"About what?"

Shelshala huddled close to Henrite to make sure no one could hear them. "Getting rid of the guards," she whispered.

After having to stay late at school, Henrite wasn't in the best of moods. "Yeah right. Didn't I tell you about the time I knocked into a guard while I was playing Tanpango in our front yard?"

Shelshala leaned away for Henrite and glared at him. "Henrite, you're nuts! You could've gotten really hurt!"

"UGH! You don't get it! My score was about to hit two million and I had to wait all day for school to finish to play again. Two million! Mikitas would have had to call me Henrite the Great for a week! I was that close." Henrite shoved his hand into Shelshala's face with two fingers about half an inch apart. He caught his breath as his shoulders slumped. "Of course, that was when we could actually play games!"

"Okay, okay. I get it. You had to play or the world would have come to an end. Calm down and lower your voice!"

"Oops, sorry."

"So what were you going to say about the guard?"

"Oh yeah, the guard," said Henrite. "So, I guess she came over to let me know I was being too loud or something and I accidently bumped into her because I had my helmet on. It felt like I'd run into a brick wall. I swear she barely felt it. Then the goon yanked off my helmet, wrote me a ticket and yelled at me to get back in the house. Two million! It makes me sick just thinking about it! I would have been the king of Tanpango!"

Henrite paused for a moment, remembering his almost moment of glory. "Anyway, there's no way we are taking anything away from the guards. They'll crack us open like clucktatos (a Kakalilian egg)!"

Shelshala continued in a whisper, "I didn't mean we would fight them. I meant we have to figure out a way to disable the Vanishers."

"Uh huh and how are we supposed to do that? Have the gun fairies sprinkle magic dust on them?"

Shelshala smirked. "Ha, Ha. Very funny. NOT. Do you really want to do this thing or not? If so, try for a lot less obnoxious and a little more helpful!"

"Okay, okay. I'm sorry. I'm just really tired." Henrite scratched his head as he thought out loud. "The Vanishers use light rays to make someone disappear...What kind of rays? Hmmm, I don't know."

"Wait! That's it! The light rays! If we figure out what kind

33

of waves they use, maybe we can figure out a way to destroy them. If we figure out how to destroy them, I am sure we can use my mom's lab to make some sort of weapon to fight the guards."

"Kaladungo! Great idea!" said Henrite. "I know! I bet we can learn how the Vanisher beams work from one of my dad's astronomy books."

Shelshala slowed down and took another quick look around to make sure no one, meaning guards, had popped up. There were only a few around in neighborhoods after kids had gotten home from school; the guards knew kids weren't allowed outside once they got home. Still, she wasn't taking any chances.

"Yes! I'm sure that will work!" Shelshala paused a second, wrinkling her nose. "But, how are we going to do all this stuff without our parents finding out?"

The kids knew that if their parents found out what they were up to, they would stop them for sure. There was no way they would let them do anything that might make them the target of a Vanisher.

"Let's just take it a step at a time," Henrite suggested. "We'll start with finding out the type of ray the guns use. No one is going to have a problem with us wanting to study even more science than we already have to. If we find out what we need to know, then we'll figure out how to get in your mom's lab."

So, just like that, they began to formulate a plan.

13

DISCOVERING A WAY
TO DESTROY A VANISHER

You may be wondering why none among the bright Kaka-lilian astronomers, physicists, chemists, biologists, mathematicians and engineers had discovered a way to fight the Vanisher. It's because Kakamuchu monitored all their activities at the universities, laboratories and companies. A monitoring screen called a Crysquid hung in every room of these types of facilities. In fact, not only were there Crysquids in all public buildings, they were also installed in the main sitting room of every Kakalilian home.

Supposedly, Crysquids were only used to transmit messages from Kakamuchu to the citizens of Kaka-La. But everyone knew they were also used for eavesdropping on them and monitoring their activities.

Also, Kakalilians were concerned that any steps they might take to oppose Kakamuchu's decrees would only make him angrier, encouraging him to do something even more terrible.

The fact that Shelshala and Henrite were kids was an incredible advantage in their plan to destroy the Vanishers. While Kakamuchu himself had been a very bright child who studied advanced science and complex math at a young age, he did not believe any of the children of Kaka-La were as smart. He just wanted children to be quiet and out of his sight. Keeping them in school from dawn to dusk was one way of accomplishing this goal. As far as he was concerned, the Royal Guards had no reason to be suspicious of children's activities. Kids were just too silly to do any harm.

So Shelshala and Henrite started planning in secret.

14

THE PLAN

To begin, Henrite and Shelshala needed a place to meet and do their research, because they could not do it at either of their homes. It had to be somewhere concealed from view, somewhere that would not make their parents wonder what they were up to.

They talked about it on their way home from school the next day, but were very careful to keep their voices low and stop talking whenever a guard flew close by.

"How about we meet in one of the bathrooms at school after everyone has gone home? There are no Crysquids there," Henrite said.

"Yuck! I'm not sitting around in the bathroom! Besides, the cleaning crew works after school."

"Oh, right. Forget it. It was a great idea. Don't know what your problem is with the bathroom. Everyone goes!"

"Whatever. Move on. That won't work. You know we're supposed to go straight home. We need somewhere without a Crysquid that our parents will actually let us go after school."

"How 'bout one of the slimeball locker rooms at the neighborhood park? No one plays anymore."

"Hmmm. That might work," said Shelshala.

Slimeball was the favorite sport on Kaka-La. A ball covered in slime was pitched to a batter and each team had its own slime color. The batter tried to hit the ball and run around three bases to home plate (a bit like in Earth baseball). Each team had four outs and there were seven innings of play. When a slimeball was caught, it was used to fling slime at a player trying to round the bases. If the slime landed on the player, he or she was out. The slime traveled very fast in the air and players had to wheel quickly, twist, turn and duck to avoid it. After a game, pretty much everyone was covered in slime. Slimeball was one more type of fun parents thought was too dangerous after the No-Laughter decree.

After thinking about meeting in the slimeball locker room a little more, Shelshala changed her mind. "No, that won't work. There are always guards in the park, even though no one goes there. They're probably just waiting until someone gets too tired of being cooped up."

"I can't think of anywhere else," said Henrite.

Shelshala was thinking so hard, she didn't see a bump in the sidewalk and tripped right over it. As she tried to regain her balance, Henrite almost laughed out loud. He barely caught himself in time.

Shelshala turned pale as a ghost as she heard his muffled laugh.

Henrite had bit down so hard on his lip that there was a drip of blood on it. He felt kind of sick to his stomach. There was a guard up ahead at the end of the street. If he had laughed...Ahh! He didn't even want to think about it.

"Henrite, are you okay?"

"Of course I'm okay!" he snapped back at her. "If you would just watch where you're going!"

Shelshala knew he wasn't mad at her, but she didn't know what to say to make him feel better. She thought a little humor might help. "Yeah, you're lucky I didn't fall flat on my face, or you would have been vanished for sure!"

A weak smile crossed Henrite's face. "Yep, I definitely would have been a goner."

They drew close to the guard and passed him in silence, continuing up the street for a couple more minutes without saying a word. It always took a while to get back to 'normal' when someone had a close call with being vanished.

Shelshala finally broke the silence. Henrite's almost getting vanished had made her think of somewhere they could meet. "I've got it! The Shrine of the Missing!"

She immediately lowered her voice to a whisper.

"No one visits the Shrine during school and work days. The guards hardly ever go up to the forest and even if someone sees us going up there, we can say it is for school. We can tell our parents we are in the forest collecting stuff for a project. I doubt they will write Mrs. Jamalku to ask her about it, as long as we don't stay out too late. How much fun can they imagine we'll be having if they think we're collecting samples of dirt and tree bark?"

"Kaladungo! Awesome idea!"

"We'll need blankets to sit on. The benches in the Shrine might be uncomfortable if we sit for a while. We'll also need lanterns. The lighting isn't very bright."

"I can bring camping lanterns."

"And, I'll bring the blankets."

They had reached their houses by this time. They agreed they would tell their parents about the 'science project'. Henrite would figure out a way to borrow a few of his father's books on physics, chemistry and astronomy to take with them to the Shrine the next day. They would also bring the lanterns and blankets in their backpacks.

"Oh and Henrite..." Shelshala said as she opened the gate into her yard.

"Yeah?"

"You'd better never get yourself vanished, 'cause when I find you, you're dead!"

"Bye, Shelshel!" He had called her Shelshel when they were babies.

Shelshala smiled. "Later!"

That night, Henrite wasn't sure how his dad would react to his wanting to borrow books. Henrite wasn't exactly the studious type and he was always complaining about schoolwork. Now, here he was about to ask for more things to study. His dad might find it odd. Now, if Shelshala asked for extra reading, his dad wouldn't be suspicious at all. "Drats", he thought. They should have had her ask. Too late now.

"Hey Dad, can I put a few of your books on my tablet? I want to read about the electromagnetic spectrum. We learned some stuff in school, but I thought your books might help me learn more."

His dad called out to his mom, "Margentie, could you bring the thermometer? I think Henrite might be sick."

"Ha, ha, Dad. Seriously. You always say I should be more curious about things beside games. Well, here I am asking. But, if you don't want me to…" Henrite started getting up from where he was sitting.

"Come on. I was just kidding. Of course you can have the books. I'll put a few on your tablet tonight."

"Thanks, Dad." Henrite headed toward the ramp to his room.

"Anytime. And son, I think it's great that something has piqued your interest. Feel free to ask me any questions you have as you are reading. Have a good night."

"Goodnight."

Mission accomplished!

15

FINALLY, A SOLUTION!

For the next two weeks, almost every day after school, Henrite and Shelshala read books about lasers. They would sit or lie on thick blankets spread on the Shrine floor and read Henrite's dad's books on their tablets by lantern light. Henrite's mom would pack them snacks, what she called 'brain food' like dark chocolate covered bodamens (a Kakalilian nut) and cheesy vegetable chips. Sometime they sat on the benches, but found the ground more comfortable for long periods of reading. By the time they left the Shrine, it would be dark. But that was no big deal, because Kakalilians had strong night vision that made being out in a dark wilderness not scary at all.

The books they read discussed the electromagnetic spectrum in much more detail than they had studied at school. They also included really cool 3-D animations of how different types of light travel through space.

Sometimes, when the kids were confused and couldn't help each other understand something, they wrote down questions to ask Henrite's dad. At first, they tried to be really careful about the types of questions they asked, so as not to make Mr. Kalamayo wonder what they were trying to find out. But after a while it became clear that Henrite's dad was so happy Henrite wanted to learn, he would have stayed up all night answering any kind of questions.

From their reading they learned that the Vanishers had to be using some kind of gamma ray, because of all the different kinds of light waves, they had the most energy. This type of wave could break apart living matter. Unfortunately, they also learned that such a strong force was nearly impossible to destroy.

Each day was filled with going to school, then the Shrine and home to eat and sleep, only to get up again and start the routine all over. They were exhausted.

"Argh, I give up!" Henrite said one day, as he threw himself down on the Shrine floor, arms spread out. "There is nothing we can do. Maybe Kakamuchu is right. Maybe we are just dumb kids who can't make anything happen. The adults who can do something are being watched all the time and we kids—who might be able to do something — don't know how! He wins! I'll just look at dirt all day and learn about ten thousand different ways people have died on other planets!"

Shelshala was sitting on a bench chewing on her hair (she always chewed on her hair when she concentrated on something or felt stressed). "Get up!" she said, throwing her drawing stylus at Henrite. As it bounced off his chest and landed on the floor, like a lightning flash in her head, Shelshala had a EUREKA! moment. She jumped up and stopped chewing on her hair.

"Henrite, get up! I've got it!"

"Leave me alone. Really, I am done! I'm going home."

Shelshala wheeled over to him and started pulling up on his arm. "Don't be such a baby! I'm telling you, I figured out what we need to do!"

Henrite slumped in a sitting position.
"Okay Ms. I-always-have-the-answer, let's hear it."

Shelshala was much too excited to get annoyed with Henrite's grumpy attitude. "What if instead of trying to destroy the ray guns, we deflect the beam?" she said. "If we could find a way to make the ray rebound and hit the guards, they'll be the ones who vanish! Not only would we be rid of the guns, but also the guards!"

She waited for Henrite to process her idea. He still looked totally defeated. Then, as her idea broke through layers of fatigue, he stopped slouching, sat up, jumped to his feet and punched Shelshala in the arm. "Kaladungo! That's absolutely brilliant!"

"OUCH!" Shelshala yelled as she rubbed her arm. "I told you never to punch me like that again!"

"I'm so sorry. It's just that it's such a great idea! You figured it out! Kakamuchu's wrong. We're not stupid!"

"Okay. Don't get so excited yet. We still have to find out if there is a way to deflect the Vanisher beam." Shelshala rubbed her sore arm. "And, Henrite Kalamayo, if you ever punch me like that again, I'm going to cause you so much pain you'll never be able to use your arm again!"

Henrite's face fell. "I'm really sorry. I just got so psyched. I mean I had totally given up. I thought there was no way out, that we would have to continue living like prisoners. Last night I even thought about doing something to get myself vanished. I thought anywhere would be better than here. But, then I remembered how miserable my parents would be."

Hearing how miserable Henrite sounded, Shelshala forgot about the pain in her arm. "I know. I feel the same way sometimes. But, hopefully, we can make something happen. We're gonna show Kakamuchu and his stupid guards that Kaka-La belongs to us!"

The friends hi-fived and gathered their things to go home.

Game on! And they were so ready for it!

16

HOW TO GET INTO THE LAB

After another week of reading chemistry and physics books, Shelshala and Henrite came across a special polymer plastic substance that, in theory, would deflect the kind of rays in the Vanisher. There was only one problem: they would have to make it. They were pretty sure all the ingredients they'd need to make the shield would be in Shelshala's mom's lab. Now, they had to figure out a way to work there without anyone noticing.

Her mom was a night owl who worked in her lab until the wee hours of the morning after everyone went to sleep. Normally, she was asleep when Shelshala and her dad left the house in the morning and would wake up in the afternoon. The kids had to figure out a way to get into the lab after she went to sleep and leave before she woke up. That meant skipping school.

They planned their strategy at the Shrine.

"Once we are in the lab, we won't have to worry about waking my mom up because it's sound-proofed. All we really have to figure out is how to get in and out of the lab without her noticing."

"We'll also have to make up an excuse not to go to school. Do you think one day will be enough to make the shield material?" asked Henrite.

"We need to do more research on how to mix the ingredients. As long as all the ingredients are in the lab, I don't think it should take more than a day."

"Just in case it does, I think the best way to skip school is to act sick. That way, staying home two or three days won't be a problem."

The weather was starting to get cold and it was chilly in the Shrine. Talking of being sick made Shelshala button up her jacket. "If we keep coming here, we may not have to lie about being sick!"

"Let's plan on getting into the lab the day after tomorrow," said Henrite. "That'll give us time to look into what order the ingredients should be mixed in so we don't blow anything up! Tomorrow we can pretend we're not feeling well at dinner and say we have sore tongues or something when we're going to bed." (Kakalilians' tongues, not their throats, get sore when they are sick.)

"That makes sense. We'll also make our tongues a little green, just to be safe. I'll bring some food coloring to school tomorrow."

"Nice detail," said Henrite. "I just can't look too sick or my mom will stay home. We also need to figure out how I'll sneak out of the house."

"Duh! That's easy. You can just come over after everyone leaves."

Henrite looked a little embarrassed. "It won't exactly be that easy."

"Oh no, Henrite! What have you done?"

"Well, this one time, when I was sick, I started feeling

better in the middle of the day. So I went to the park and played slimeball with some other kid who also hadn't gone to school. By the time we finished playing, I was REALLY sick and dragged slime all the way through the house to my bed. I thought my dad was going to ground me for life. They cleaned all the slime with your mom's Slime-Out machine, but now, if I stay home sick, my mom and dad check on me a gazillion times on the Crysquid." (Kakalilians could use one of the channels of the Crysquid for video-conferencing into their homes.)

"Okay then, you have to look like you're home..." Shelshala said as she wheeled across the Shrine to stay warm.

"And Crysquid available," Henrite added.

"Hmmm, we could make up a bed on the couch in front of the Crysquid. A blanket covering a few pillows should make it look like you're asleep with your head covered."

"That's not going to stop them from trying to talk with me. They might check to see if I'm awake under the covers."

"Snoring," mumbled Shelshala.

"What! I do not snore!"

"Please. When I come over to your house for sleepovers, I bring ear plugs!"

Henrite squirmed a little. "Okay, maybe I snore every once in a while. I see where you're going with that. I'll record myself sleeping tonight and we can put the recording under the blanket. Just don't blame me if I don't snore."

Shelshala knew there was no chance that was going to happen! But, she didn't say anything to irritate Henrite. He agreed to the idea and that was all that mattered.

So the plan was set. Henrite would set things up at his house and then they would go to Shelshala's mom's lab to begin work on the deflector material. They both felt really excited as well as nervous, especially about fooling their parents. Neither of them liked the idea of lying, but there was just no other way to get the plan in motion.

17

MAKING THE
DEFLECTOR SHIELD

It worked! Shelshala and Henrite convinced their parents that they were sick and got to stay home from school! Although, the green dye they used to color their tongues to look sick almost worked too well. Henrite's tongue was so green his mom insisted on staying home with him.

"Mom, you don't have to stay home. I can take care of myself. I already feel better."

Mrs. Kalamayo looked doubtful. "I don't know, Henrite. I'm afraid you'll try to get up before you should."

"MOM, I won't do that again! Come on. You've gotta trust me. I'm older now."

Henrite's dad was at the front door, putting his coat on. "Margentie, he'll be fine. You can check on him to make sure he's not doing anything crazy."

"Oh alright, you boys win! Make sure you eat the soup the Grubster is making and liquids...don't forget to drink juice throughout the day. She fluffed his pillow, pulled the blanket up to his chin and kissed his forehead. "I will be checking on you!"

"And I will be right here, bored out of my mind! That's nothing new!"

"Bye, Henrite."

"Bye, Mom."

Henrite felt a tinge of guilt about deceiving his parents. Then he reminded himself that he and Shelshala weren't doing all this for fun. They weren't even having any fun! Well, maybe a little. But, that didn't count because what they were really trying to do was monumental! Their parents would understand that. Well, hopefully they would understand. He would be really bummed if they got upset with him.

Henrite waited for about ten minutes after his mom left with his sister before turning on the recorder under the blankets, changing out of his PJs and heading over to Shelshala's house.

When he got there, Shelshala was waiting at the door so he wouldn't have to knock.

"How'd it go?"

"Argh! My mom treats me like I'm three! She trusts my pipsqueak sister more than me! She was gonna stay home. My dad and I finally got her to leave. But she has soup grubbing and she expects me to be drinking juice all day. She wants me to stay in bed, but apparently it's okay for me to have to get up and pee all day!"

"That's not a problem. Around lunchtime, we'll go over to your house and put an empty bowl of soup and a half empty bottle of Talaka juice (Kakalilian orange juice) on the table in front of the couch. You can go back again a little later and drink the rest of the juice. I'll set an alarm on my tablet so we don't forget."

Henrite threw his arms up in exasperation. "Here we are trying to save the planet and all my mom can think about is soup!"

Shelshala raised her finger to her lips. "Shhh! You're gonna wake my mom!"

Once they were in the lab, they started looking through the array of chemicals. One wall was lined with bottles of different chemicals, minerals and salts. Along another wall, was a selection of metallic and plastic materials. They did not anticipate having any trouble locating all the ingredients they needed for the deflector, because all the containers were clearly labeled.

Not wanting to waste any time, they started working. They knew the guards would either be watching or taping the lab through the Crysquid. But Shelshala and Henrite were not too concerned about that. After all, kids were still kids. Even on dreary Kaka-La, playing hooky to investigate a lab full of interesting stuff would not appear that out of the ordinary. They did make sure to keep talking about how they would be in big trouble if their parents found out what they were up to, just to make sure the guards would not get suspicious. They had also memorized all the ingredients for the deflector so it wouldn't be necessary to look at any notes.

"We'll be in major trouble if we get caught!" Shelshala said as she picked up different sized beakers from a shelf within arms reach under one of the work tables. There were already hot plates, burners and other equipment in open containers lined up on the table.

"I know. But it will be worth it! I'm so sick of school. At least in your mom's lab we can have some fun. What's this funny looking thing?" Henrite pointed at a cap with a bunch of wires sticking out of. It had been pushed back in a cabinet.

"Don't you remember? For a while, most of the ponggies in our neighborhood walked around with these caps on their heads. My mom thought she might be able to help ponggies talk by translating their thoughts into words."

"Totally! How could I forget? Kalabbie looked so ridiculous. He didn't need words to tell us, 'Help! Get this thing off me!'"

"Yeah, poor ponggies! She finally gave up on the idea when a few of them kept falling over on their faces from the weight of the cap!"

Henrite sat on one of the lab stools and swiveled around. "So, what should we do? How 'bout mixing some stuff together? Maybe we'll come up with something cool!"

"Okay, that sounds like fun. You bring me stuff, and I'll mix."

"How come you get to mix? I wanna mix, too!"

"I don't think so. Remember when you almost blew up the science lab because you didn't follow directions about which chemicals not to mix together?"

"Oh yeah, right. Okay, you mix. I'll find cool looking stuff to mix."

Henrite gathered the first set of ingredients for the shield. He picked up a few non-shield related chemicals and salts as well, just to be safe.

Shelshala put on protective glasses and started combining the shield ingredients. They knew what chemicals shouldn't be mixed directly together. They also had figured out the sequence in which the ingredients should be blended.

For a couple of chemical combinations they were unsure how long they needed to wait before adding the next set of ingredients. They were just going to have to make adjustments as needed along the way.

Everything was going pretty smoothly until Shelshala cried out, "Oh No!" She grabbed the fire extinguisher from under the table to hose down a beaker in front of her...

18

M E L T D O W N !

"What happened?" Henrite rushed to the table. One of the beakers had smoke coming out of it with a murky black gooey substance inside.

"It's okay." Shelshala tilted her head down towards the smoking beaker. "The mixture of chemicals I added caused a fire." She picked up a glove that was magnetized to stick to the table rim and used it to take the beaker off the burner. "Once it cools down, could you wash the beaker out in the hazardous waste sink, just to be safe?"

"Sure thing," said Henrite.

"I'll start over again. Looks like we need to wait longer before adding the two mixtures together," said Shelshala. Then she quickly added (just in case anyone might be listening through the Crysquid): "I'm not really sure that will work, but we can try it."

Shelshala started combining the chemicals over again and Henrite worked at cleaning the beaker. When Shelshala got to the point where the chemical mixture had caught fire before, instead of waiting in the lab for it to stabilize, she and Henrite headed over to his house. They were both really hungry. Henrite got under the covers on the couch and ate the soup from the Grubster. Shelshala ate in the kitchen outside of Crysquid view. Their timing was perfect; Henrite's mom checked in on him as he was eating.

"Henrite?" (Mrs. Kalamayo appeared on the Crysquid screen.)

"Hi, mom." Henrite glanced quickly towards the kitchen to make sure Shelshala was nowhere in sight.

"Hi Love. Good, I see you're eating your soup. How are you feeling?"

"Better."

"Where were you earlier? I kept calling your name and you didn't answer."

"I was here, asleep under the covers."

"Oh, I see. I thought I heard snoring, but wasn't sure. Remember, even though you are feeling better, stay in bed. Are you drinking liquids? I'll be home in a few hours. Maybe I'll cancel my last class."

"No, mom! Stop treating me like a baby!! I'm good and eating my soup, see." Henrite lifted a spoon full of soup to his mouth."

Mrs. Kalamayo was unconvinced.

"Why did you change out of your pajamas?" (When Henrite had leaned forward to eat the soup, the blanket had fallen off his shoulder.)

He had to think fast.

"Okay, you got me. I did get up. I didn't want to forget to put out the recycling bin. So when it crossed my mind while I was lying here doing nothing, I did it."

The energy plants like the one Henrite's dad worked at were responsible for energy conservation through the "Don't Waste a Star" Program. Every month, each Kakalilian home was given an allotment of star-energy based on their needs. Once a month, all electrical appliances, outlets and switches in each home were automatically examined for energy use. Any items not using energy efficiently were identified for repair or recycling. Electrical technicians were immediately sent out to make repairs. Items that could not be repaired and needed replacing were put in a recycling bin for pickup. Everybody got coupons to buy replacements. Henrite was responsible for putting the bin out at his house and he was notoriously known for forgetting.

"You changed out of your pajamas for that?" asked Henrite's mom.

"Of course I did! I'm not going out in public with my pajamas on!"

Mrs. Kalamayo smiled. "All right then. Don't go out again. I'll check back in with you in the afternoon. Bye for now."

Her image disappeared from the screen.

Shelshala waited a few seconds and then came into the sitting room with a bottle of Talaka juice.

Henrite had thrown the covers off and was sitting up on the sofa. "See. What'd I tell you? Just like I'm still three!"

"Come on. It wasn't that bad. And, it's not like you're Mr. Innocent."

"Geeze, that was a long time ago!"

"Anyway, it was great how you came up with the recycling bin thing," said Shelshala as she gave the bottle of juice to Henrite. "Hurry and drink half of this."

Henrite chugged down the juice and handed the bottle back to Shelshala.

She put it on the table beside the sofa while Henrite rearranged the pillows and blankets for the make believe bed.

As they headed out of the house, Henrite remembered the recycling bin.

"Wait a sec. I need to put out the recycling bin or I'm gonna have to answer another thousand questions when my mom gets home!

Once they were back in the lab, they had another setback. One of the salt compounds Shelshala added melted the soft plastic-like substance that was beginning to form.

"How'd that happen?" Henrite asked.

"I'm not sure. Somehow, adding this salt brought down the melting point."

With his back to the Crysquid, Henrite threw Shelshala a look of warning.

She got the message. She must not sound so knowledgeable about chemicals. "At least, I guess that's what happened. Remember when Mrs. Jamalku babbled on and on about melting and freezing points."

"No way, I tune that stuff out. Who cares? So does this mean we wasted our time for nothing?" asked Henrite.

"Maybe not. We can try it one more time. It was starting to turn into something soft and plastic-y."

"Awesome. Maybe we can make fake laser guns."

"That's a dumb idea. I'm going to make a sculpture and try heating it in the oven until it hardens. Then, I'll show it to your mom to see what she thinks," said Shelshala.

"Whatever. You make a ridiculous sculpture and I'll make a gun, assuming we actually have something to work with."

"Right. Let's try adding something else instead of this stuff," Shelshala said, pointing to the bottle of the salt compound she had just added.

She wheeled over to where the bottles of salts were sitting along the wall. When she got to the empty space where the salt that had caused the meltdown had sat, she noticed another bottle behind the one Henrite had picked up. She took it back to the table to compare it. The second bottle had a slightly different chemical formula written on the label. The difference was barely noticeable. Hopefully, it was a big enough difference to explain the meltdown.

Two hours later, all the ingredients had been combined together without any more fires or meltdowns. They had made a transparent soft plastic material that could be molded into different shapes.

Shelshala and Henrite were totally psyched, but very careful not to show it. They had no idea if the substance would actually work as a deflector, but at least it looked like it was supposed to. They played around with it for a little while, shaping it into a ball and throwing it back and forth and holding on to the ends and pulling it apart to see how far it would stretch.

They had both lost track of time when the clock on the wall caught Henrite's attention. "Drats, we need to get outta here! Your mom'll be getting up any second."

Shelshala started to panic. "She's probably already up and taking a shower! Hurry! Let's hide this stuff until we can get back in the lab another day."

They rolled the material up and Shelshala hid it behind a container in the corner of the lab. Henrite had already put away all the ingredients they'd used, so the lab was pretty much back to normal as far as they could tell. They took one more look around and headed out.

They had done it! Their plan was not just a plan any more. There was no turning back now.

19

THAT EVENING AT HOME

That night at dinner, Dr. Kakachala was a bit confused.

"I could swear some of my chemical bottles are not as full as I remember them being."

She was a little absentminded, especially when she was working on a new invention. So when Mr. Kakachala responded, "Do not worry, dear. I am sure it is just a trick of the eye," Shelshala's mom shrugged her shoulders.

"You are most likely right," she said. "I know I get a little too involved with my experiments sometimes. Maybe I used the chemicals and don't remember."

Shelshala kept her head down and ate her salad.

"Shelshala?" asked her dad.

She lifted her head. "Yes, Dad?"

"Hmmm, you're really enjoying that salad!" he said.

"Oh, I'm just hungry after resting all day."

She could tell her dad was unconvinced by her response (or her quick recovery), but he did not ask her anything else. She and Henrite would have to be very careful. If either of their parents got a sense that anything was going on, the plan was done for!

20

MORE THINKING
LEADS TO A NEW STRATEGY

After school the next day, Shelshala and Henrite went to
the Shrine to talk about the next steps of their plan: mainly,
how in the world they were going to test the shield material
without taking the risk of someone being vanished.

"I'll do it!" offered Henrite.

"No way! If you get vanished, I won't need to be vanished
because your parents will kill me. Either we test it together
or figure out some other way."

"I know it will be hard, but maybe we can find a laughing
toy, like we used to have when we were kids," said Henrite.
"We can put it somewhere outside and cover it with the
deflector material. The goons always shoot first and ask
questions later. When they hear the laughing toy and shoot
it, we'll find out if the shield works."

"And if it doesn't disappear?" said Shelshala. "Then what?
The guards will know something's up. They'll examine
the toy."

"Oh...yeah...hadn't thought of that," said Henrite.
"So we're back to me wearing the shield!"

"NO!" said Shelshala. "Even if you wear the shield and
the guard who shoots you disappears, another guard will

grab you. Everyone will be put under house arrest until they figure out what is going on."

Henrite frowned. "UGH. This sucks! We may have found a way to save everyone, but we can't even test it!"

"We're not giving up that easily! But I do think we're going to have to let our parents in on it now. They'll be able to tell us if the shield will work. It looks as if whatever we do, everyone will be at risk. So everyone has a right to know the plan. Then they can decide for themselves if they want us to try the shield. Otherwise we're no better than Kakamuchu, making decisions for other people."

"There's no way adults will let us!"

"We don't know that for sure," said Shelshala. "Adults were kids once and they hate the No-Laughter decree as much as we do. Maybe they're as tired as we are of being told what to do! And don't forget, if the Vanished are still alive, they might be somewhere with little food or shelter. I asked my mom and she told me, worst-case scenario, if they were transported to a planet that doesn't have conditions for survival, they can hibernate with no water, food, or air for about six months. If there is any chance that we can save them, we have to find them NOW."

Henrite was convinced. "Okay! Let's do it! How about right now? You can have your parents come over to my house."

"Not yet. Let's figure out our plan for vanishing the guards first, so we have a strategy before talking with them."

"You're right. My dad is always on my case for not 'thinking things through'. It's just that I REALLY want to blow those guards to smithereens!"

"Watch out, that's the kind of talk that's going to get you an injection of anti-aggression serum!" warned Shelshala.

"Ha ha! There's no such thing! Adults just made that up to scare us!" said Henrite.

"There is so! I talked with Mikitas and Mattchu the day after they had a shoving match in class. The school nurse totally gave them a shot of anti-aggression serum—in their butts! They told me after they got the shot, for about three hours, all they felt like doing was hugging each other. They kept as far away from each other as they could for the rest of the day!"

"I don't know…I don't buy it," Henrite said. "Either way, you're right. If it sounds like all we want to do is vaporize the guards because we're mad, our parents won't let us. So, what's the plan?"

Shelshala chewed on her hair. "I think that somehow, everyone will have to wear a shield. If it works, everybody can start laughing to get all the guards shooting at the same time. That's the only way to vanish all of them at once."

"Makes sense," said Henrite.

"How do we make sure everyone knows the plan though?" asked Shelshala.

They were silent for a while, thinking.

"I know!" yelled Henrite. "Kenakada! He knows tons about computer systems. I bet he can break into the Crysquid network without the thugs knowing. We can flash a quick message into everyone's house explaining the plan."

"That's a fabulous idea!!" said Shelshala, but then her shoulders slumped. "Double UGH, how do we get everyone on the planet a shield?"

They were really bummed out by this question. The good news was that most of the planet was uninhabited. There was the capital, where they lived, and two neighboring cities called Kakamuchuphile I and Kakamuchuphile II. The rest of the planet was protected nature habitats.

The bad news was that still meant a lot of shields.

"Okay, let's not get bummed out!" said Shelshala. "I think we've come up with enough details that our parents will know we've thought our plan through. Let's talk to Kenakada tomorrow. We'll have to swear him to secrecy. Once we're sure he can intercept the Crysquid transmission, we'll share the plan with our parents. I know they'll be able to help us with the missing steps."

So they wrote out their plan on a piece of paper to give to Kenakada the next day, ending the note with DESTROY AFTER READING in bold letters.

"I'll put it in his backpack when no one's looking," Shelshala said as she slipped the note into her jacket pocket. "I can't wait to see the reaction on his face after he reads it!"

"Please, this is Kenakada we're talking about. The only way he would get excited is if the plan promised he could stay home fooling around on his tablet all day!"

Shelshala chuckled a little. (There were no guards to be found in the Shrine!) "That might be true. But, let's hope he'll help us, or we're going to have to figure out another way—and my brain could really use a break!"

21

KENAKADA'S RESPONSE

The next day, Shelshala pretended to trip over Kenakada's backpack and slipped the note into its front pocket. As Kenakada leaned down to help her up, their heads hit. He turned bright green (Kakalilians turn green when they are embarrassed) and she quickly returned to her seat.

Mrs. Jamalku always wore a really loud horn around her neck, which she would blow whenever anything funny happened in class to remind kids not to laugh and to immediately cover the sound of any laughter that may have already started. Kenakada and Shelshala's collision was definitely a 'horn moment.'

Kenakada didn't say anything the next day, or the day after. Shelshala and Henrite had no idea if he had read the note or not. He didn't act any differently toward them. They could not take the chance of asking him anything at school, because someone might overhear them and wonder what they were talking about.

Finally, on the third day, when Shelshala was putting on her jacket to head home from school, she felt a piece of paper in the front pocket. She was dying to open it! But to be safe, she waited until she got home.

The note, in bold letters, said: YES I CAN AND I AM IN!

After reading the note, Shelshala headed over to Henrite's house. The door opened seconds before she got to it. Henrite must have been waiting right behind it.

She didn't go in. "Hey, just wanted to let you know that Kenakada wants to join our study group."

Henrite couldn't help pumping his fist. "Awesome!"

"We can plan a meeting time with him tomorrow."

"Works for me."

"Later."

Shelshala waited until the door close, danced a quick jig and headed back home.

22

MEETING WITH KENAKADA

The next day they needed to get a note about meeting at the Shrine directly into Kenakada's hands. They couldn't leave it in his backpack like last time, because he might not read it in time to meet the following day.

Luck had it that, in the middle of math class, Kenakada raised his hand to go to the bathroom. Two kids were allowed to go to the bathroom at the same time, so just as Kenakada left the room, Shelshala's hand shot up and she asked to be excused too. By the time she got permission and was in the hall, Kenakada was heading into the boys' bathroom. She couldn't just stand there waiting for him. A teacher might pass by and ask her what she was doing. So she decided to follow him into the bathroom. If someone was in there with him, she would just act as if she'd made a mistake. But, if he was alone, she would hand him the note and leave.

When Shelshala appeared in the bathroom, Kenakada lost his balance and fell back, landing on his behind with a loud thud. "Ouch!"

Shelshala ignored his pain and startled expression and wheeled across the restroom, checking under all the stalls. Once she was sure there was no one in the bathroom but Kenakada, she wheeled back and put the note into his hand.

He still sat on the floor with a dumbfounded expression on his face. Then, she headed back to class. By the time Kenakada came back to class, he was his normal cool self.

He showed up at the cave the next day as arranged.

"Nice hideout. I am majorly impressed with you guys's plan. I've been trying to figure out a way to jam the guards' computer system for a while. I've gotten to a point where I get into the system for about five minutes before their warning system tags me as unauthorized."

"How have you gotten away with it? What happens when you're detected?" asked Henrite.

Kenakada smiled slyly. "Well, when they detect me, I redirect to one of the data centers where they collect information. Makes them go into lockdown mode to see if anyone unauthorized has gotten into the building."

"So all the times the yellow security alarms have been activated, it's been because of you?" asked Shelshala.

"I wouldn't say all the times."

"Very cool," said Henrite. "I never would have guessed it was you."

"That's the whole point. But after reading you guys's plan, I get that there was no way I could have done anything on my own. They vanished my cousin with the whole No-Laughter thing. I'll try anything to find him."

"Oh, I'm so sorry, Kenakada! I had no idea!" said Shelshala.

Kenakada looked uncomfortable with the sympathy. "Yeah, I don't really like talking about it. Let's just get to work on the plan."

Henrite quickly changed the subject. "Sure. How long can you get us into the Crysquid system?"

"Like I said, about five minutes. When were you planning on doing the transmission? I need a little time to tag all the Crysquids in public and security buildings so the message doesn't get routed to those systems."

"Of course! Good thing you thought of that!" said Henrite. "We still have to tell our parents about the plan and work out some details with them." Henrite didn't share with Kenakada the possibility that their parents might nix the plan. "I imagine it will be at least another two weeks before we're ready." He looked over at Shelshala for confirmation.

"Or longer," she said. "How long do you think you'll need?"

"It's a centralized system. Two weeks should be plenty of time," said Kenakada. "Kakamuchu thinks he's all that when it comes to the security system, but there are holes galore in it!"

"Perfect," said Shelshala. "So you start working on identifying the Crysquids. Me and Henrite will work on the rest. Once everything is ready to go on our end, we'll let you know."

"Works for me. Just say when."

So, another step of the plan was in place.

Now, for the parents!

23

OH BOY, NOW THE PARENTS

Shelshala and Henrite were pretty sure their parents would help out. But you just never know with parents. Sometimes you think you're going to get into a lot of trouble for doing something and they'll just tell you not to do it again. Other times, when you think you're going to get off easy, they explode—like the time Henrite tied his little sister's feet together when she was learning how to wheel.

Both of them were pretty sure their parents wouldn't be mad about them lying and working in the lab once they understood why they'd done it. The problem was the plan itself. Their parents might absolutely forbid them to move forward with it. But then what? Back to no fun and being watched all the time?

At the Shrine they discussed the details of how to get the plan to their parents.

"We'll need to use notes," said Shelshala.

"Yeah, but we can't just hand them a random note. They might ask what it's about in front of the Crysquid. How about mailing them?"

"No way! Mail gets scanned for suspicious words."

"Oh, yeah."

Shelshala chewed on her hair. "Notes, notes...what other

kind of notes do parents get?"

Henrite had started playing "Bat-an-Eye" when they got to the Shrine. Each time the ball made contact with the paddle in his hand it grew smaller. It started about the size of an Earth tennis ball and gradually decreased to the size of a gnat. Kakalilians had really strong eyesight and no problem seeing the ball as it got smaller. The challenge was in the ball rebounding faster and faster after making contact with the paddle.

As he talked with Shelshala, Henrite concentrated on the movement of the ball, his eyes darting up and down faster and faster.

"Henrite! Are you listening to me?"

"Uh huh," he mumbled, moving the paddle around to hit the ball.

Shelshala grabbed the ball midair.

"Hey. What the...give me the ball back!" Henrite demanded.

"No! You need to pay attention! This isn't a time for playing!"

"And since when are you Royal Guard of Bat-an-Eye!"

"That's a stupid thing to say! What's the big deal? You can play later."

"I wanna play now!" Henrite reached out to grab the ball out of Shelshala's hand, accidently scratching her as she pulled her arm away from him.

"Ouch! That hurt!" Shelshala yelled. "Fine, have it your way! Play your stupid game!" She got up from the floor and started stuffing the blanket she had been sitting on in her backpack. "I don't care if you play until you're cross-eyed! I'm out of here! Figure out what to do with the notes yourself!"

"Come on, don't be such a baby!"

Shelshala swung her backpack on her shoulder and turned sharply around to him. "I might be a baby. But, I'm not an insensitive buffoon who plays games HERE. Everything isn't always about you!" Then she wheeled passed him and left the Shrine.

Henrite was left standing by himself. His eyes wandered across the walls and a feeling of guilt crept up on him. He had always been so busy reading or planning when they were in the Shrine that he hadn't been paying much attention to the walls. Now, as he scanned the pictures of all the Vanished, covering the walls from top to bottom and in some places five pictures thick, he remembered it was not too long ago that there had been a lot of empty spaces.

He moved closer to one wall and caught a glimpse of a familiar face towards the ground. He bent down to get a closer look and saw Kalamoo, one of their classmates who had vanished the first week of the No-Laughter decree. He was the kid in class who always cracked jokes and made everyone laugh. Once the decree was made effective, all the adults had kept an eye on him and constantly reminded him not to crack jokes. But, it was no use. There was no way he could remember all the time.

Henrite felt like a real idiot. Of all places, how could he have been playing in the Shrine? What was he thinking! He was the one acting like a little kid. Shelshala was right and now she was mad at him. He was going to have to eat some major crow.

He heard a sound at the Shrine entrance.
Shelshala was back.

"Sorry I lost my temper," she said. He could tell she was still peeved.

"Are you kidding me? You were so right. I was an idiot. What was I thinking playing here? I'm really sorry, Shel."

She could never resist a genuine apology. "Let's just forget it. We're both exhausted. Between school, planning and real homework, there's no time left for anything."

"Yeah. I definitely could use a break," Henrite said with a smile. "But, this isn't about me. It's about this place, Kalamoo and Kenakada's cousin. Doing what's right. Thanks for a much needed reminder."

"Okay then, let's get back to the notes." Shelshala moved over to one of the benches closest to them, sat down and put her backpack on the floor.

"Any thoughts?"

Henrite sat next to her. "Hmmm, most everything is done through tablets. Wait. I know: "Spread the Joy" notes. Teachers give them to us instead of messaging our parents." "Spread The Joy" notes let parents know when their child scored very high on an examination or did something really nice for someone.

"That's right! The notes that your parents hardly ever get!" teased Shelshala.

"Whatever, Ms. Teacher's Pet."

"I am not a teacher's pet! I can't help it if I actually like learning!"

"Just admit it's MY great idea."

"Okay, YOUR great idea," said Shelshala. "You need to have one every few hundred years!"

"Ha ha. You're SO funny."

They took out their tablets and wrote out the notes, making sure they included every detail of the plan. They would print them when they got home. After they finished writing, all that was left was to borrow a "Spread the Joy" stamp off a teacher's desk and stamp the front of their notes.

Tomorrow night the notes would be in their parents' hands. They wished each other luck and headed home.

24

THE PARENTS RESPOND

The next evening, right before dinner, they handed over their notes. They knew their parents would read them after the kids had gone to bed. As a rule, they did not like to interrupt family time.

Henrite was anxiously sitting up in bed when his dad and mom came to his room. His dad gave him a big hug. "In case we forget to tell you sometimes, we are really proud of you! I know you have some questions about your science lesson that we didn't have time to get to today. I'll put together some notes for you." Even though they were in Henrite's room, no one was sure what the Crysquid range was for picking up voices, so Henrite's dad acted like he was talking about a 'lesson' when he was really talking about the kids' plan.

Then, holding back her tears, his mom hugged him so hard Henrite thought his dinner was going to come back up as projectile vomit.

"It was so sweet of you to help the little boy at school." She was clearly playing along with the pretend "Spread the Joy" note. "I am going to talk with Shelshala's mom tomorrow after work and see if she has any special glue that will prevent the little boy's artificial eyeball from popping out again."

"Ha ha, very funny, Mom," thought Henrite. He wasn't sure what his mom was going to talk to Dr. Kakachala about, but it didn't matter. All that mattered was that they were in. His parents were going to help with the plan!

At Shelshala's house, things did not go quite as smoothly.

Her mom came to her room without her dad: not a good sign.

"Great job on your test, honey. I'll review your answers in the lab tonight and see if there is any additional reading I can recommend. Sorry your dad didn't come up to say goodnight. The kitchen-cleaning robot isn't working properly and he's tinkering with it."

As she leaned over to kiss Shelshala goodnight, she whispered, "I will work on your dad."

So her dad was not happy with the plan. Shelshala knew he was overprotective and didn't want her in any kind of danger. She also knew that if her mom could not convince him to move forward with the plan, there was no way she could stay involved.

Shelshala was so mad and sad at the same time, she felt like crying. It was so unfair! She wasn't really mad at her dad, just mad at the whole situation. Why did Kakamuchu have to be so terrible? Why were Kakalilians such gentle and kind people that let him get away with it? Why wasn't she an adult who had finished university and knew enough science to figure out how to test the shield herself?

Her mom, knowing that Shelshala would have trouble sleeping, quietly sprayed a calming mist in her room after tucking her in. As Shelshala dozed off, she hoped Henrite had had better luck at his house.

25

A CHANGE OF HEART

From the wide grin on Henrite's face the next day at school, Shelshala knew he had good news. Her looks — chewed off hair and post-calming-mist-drowsiness — let him know things had not gone so well at her house. Of course they could not talk about it until after school, and school took FOREVER.

Henrite felt really bad for Shelshala. Nothing would suck more than if her dad nixed her involvement with the plan. On their way home, he tried as best he could to lift her spirits.

"Shel, my mom said she was going to talk with your mom today. They'll totally gang up on your dad. He doesn't stand a chance."

Shelshala still looked like someone had punched her in the gut.

"And, if there is even the slimmest chance that he won't give into them," Henrite continued, "my dad will convince him. We've got three out of four, Shel! There's no way it's not happening!"

"Yeah. I guess so. But, if my dad's made up his mind, there's no way I can be part of it. I know I should be happy that everything will happen with or without me. It isn't about me, but..." Shelshala was very close to crying, so she stopped talking.

"Nothing's going to happen without you! I know what I'm talking about. Our moms and my dad are on board. Your dad will give in!"

"We'll see," Shelshala said with a sigh.

They were getting close to their houses.

"Do you want me to come in with you?" asked Henrite.

"No thanks. I prefer experiencing misery on my own."

"Trust me. It's not going to play out the way you're thinking."

"Thanks, Henrite. Sorry for being such a downer. See ya tomorrow."

"Later."

As Shelshala entered her house, she could hear voices in the kitchen. The moms were sitting together having a cup of Lakteala (Kakalilian tea), looking as normal as ever.

"How can they be so calm?" Shelshala wondered as she threw her backpack and jacket in the closet by the front door and wheeled toward the kitchen.

Mrs. Kalamayo got up to give her a hug. "Shelshala, so good to see you. Your mom and I were just chatting away and let the time get away from us." She whispered in Shelshala's ear, "Your mom has something to share with you that I know will make you very happy!"

In a normal voice she continued, "I'm heading out now. It's Henrite's dad's turn to make dinner. Thank goodness for your mom's Grubster! He always has his head in books. We would go hungry every other day if he actually had to prepare something! Toddles!"

Henrite's mom left and Shelshala's mom cleared the cups from the table. She smiled up at Shelshala.

"Hmmm, hair all chewed up? Are you out of your Quick Hair Growth cream? Do you need me to whip you up some more?"

"No, I just forgot."

"Well. You may want to put some on and try not to look like a nervous wreck when your dad gets home. He is enough of a nervous wreck for all of us. You know how overprotective he is. He is definitely going to be losing a lot of sleep over you wanting to learn how to super turbo-charge your wheels for racing."

For a second Shelshala had no idea what her mom was talking about, but then it clicked. She almost knocked her mother over as she hugged her.

"Whoa! Whoa! You may not want to injure me," her mom teased. "I'm the one who has to help you maximize your turbo powered chargers without sending you rocketing into a wall!"

That meant her mom was going to work on the shield! But how? Shelshala felt her heart sink to her knees. The guards were always watching her mom's lab. What if they figured out what she was doing? All this was just becoming too stressful for a kid!

After hugging Shelshala back, her mom said, "It is amazing what a group of people can do when they put their heads together. Henrite's mom told me his dad is working on the best angle to apply the turbo charging. Once we figure out how to make sure it's powerful enough to get the job done, he'll let us know where to apply it on your team's wheels. It's all going to work out just fine."

So the Kakamuchu Speed Relay Race was going to be code for the plan! With all the stuff going on in Shelshala's head, she had almost forgotten all about the race. Their parents were so smart to use it as a code for the plan! The race was happening in about two months. Kids always got very excited about preparations and the goon guards would not be surprised to hear them talking about it all the time.

Shelshala's mom pushed her toward the kitchen entryway. "Go put some cream on!"

Shelshala was so happy wheeling up the ramp to her room. But also a little scared. What if it didn't work? What if they were all vanished? No. No. Stop that, she admonished herself. Only positive thoughts!

26

UGH, MORE WAITING

Henrite and Shelshala hadn't heard anything from their parents about the plan for over a week.

Henrite had just about had it. He shared his frustration on their way home from school.

"Urgh! If I knew planning required so much waiting, I totally would not have started working on this thing in the first place! There has got to be something we can do, instead of just waiting. Maybe we should write our parents another note to hurry up already!"

"I know. It's driving me crazy, too! But, we've just gotta keep remembering they're adults. They're gonna have to be a lot more careful about doing anything that may look out of the ordinary. We get away with a lot because we're kids."

"I know! I know!" Henrite's frustration made him speed down the street.

"Slow down! You're going to get stopped!" Shelshala yelled, as he sped ahead of her.

Just as the words came out of Shelshala's mouth, a guard appeared out of nowhere on his motokalin and came up behind Henrite. "Reduce your speed or be fined!" he yelled at Henrite through his blastocom (a Kakalilian voice amplifier).

Shelshala, who was a few feet behind Henrite, jumped in fright and almost lost her balance. He slowed down. The guard flew up right above him to intimidate him. Henrite stopped in his tracks and glared up at the guard.

By this time, Shelshala had caught up. She grabbed Henrite under his arm and kept moving. "Sorry, sir. It won't happen again!" she yelled. To Henrite she whispered between her teeth, "Don't be an idiot. Keep moving!"

The guard continued moving above them for about half a minute and then blasted ahead down the street.

Shelshala could feel Henrite fuming beside her. She was shaking with fear and anger.

They didn't say another word as they wheeled the rest of the way home. There was always a chance the guard might make another round.

As they reached Shelshala's front gate, she turned to Henrite and glared. "You really do dumb things sometimes!" She wheeled up to her house, went inside and slammed the door behind her.

Henrite kicked his front gate open. His mom had clearly heard Shelshala yelling at him and opened the front door before he got to it. "Please don't knock the door down. We need it for a while! What happened?"

Henrite was still really mad. "The goon guard! I'm not afraid of them with their brainless heads and pumped up bodies! I don't care if they vanish me! I hate them! They're just a bunch of bullies!"

Henrite's mom let him vent a bit. "Now honey," she said glancing behind her at the Crysquid, "I know it can be frustrating at times, but you know the guards are here for our protection and security. We are lucky to have them."

Henrite saw his mom looking at the Crysquid and calmed down a bit. "Sorry Mom, I was just tired from school and wanted to get home as quickly as I could."

"Okay then. Why don't you go up to your room and rest a little before dinner? I'm going to make a quick trip next door to see how Shelshala is doing." She gave him a kiss on top of his head and headed out the front door.

Now that he had calmed down, Henrite felt like a real idiot. To get in trouble now—what was he thinking! Sometimes he just couldn't help it. He got so mad. Who knows what might have happened if Shelshala hadn't been there. He really needed to control his temper or else he could ruin everything!

27

HENRITE'S DAD'S NOTE

Finally, a few days later, as he was taking his tablet out
of his backpack at school, Henrite found a note. He and
Shelshala paid absolutely no attention during their
lessons and headed straight for the Shrine after school.

When they got there, Henrite read the note out loud:

Hi, Son.

*Sorry I missed you at breakfast this morning. I have
been thinking about the race. We definitely want to
make sure each of your team members' turbochargers
are adjusted for their feet size. I have figured out the
best way to accomplish this.*

*After you guys and Shelshala's mom finish the final
touches on the turbocharger (by the way, you both did
an amazing job researching turbochargers!), she will add
an accelerator that will only work for your team. It will
not work on the other teams. Remember how all Kakalilians
share similar cell types, which make up their bodies?
Well, Shelshala's mom is going to add something to the
turbochargers so they will only bond with your team's feet,
grow to the size of each team member's foot and stay on
no matter how hard racers from other teams try to break
them off.*

As a science lesson for you and Shelshala, Dr. Kakachala is going to have you guys work on the special cover for the turbochargers. A list of ingredients for the cover is included at the end of this note. Work on it when you get a chance and let Dr. Kakachala know when you are done.

Also, you forgot to put out the energy bin again. What if everyone neglects to put their bins out for recycling?

Dad

"I get the first part," said Shelshala. "My mom is adding something to the shield material so the shields will only bond with Kakalilians' bodies and not Royal Guards, because they're not the same species we are. But I still don't get how we're getting the shields to everyone."

They both silently read the note again.

After she finished reading, Shelshala said, "I also don't get what energy bins have to do with anything."

Henrite's face lit up. "Kaladungo! That's it! The energy bins! Every house gets a pickup and replacement of their recycling bin once a month. The shields will be put in the replacement bins!"

"Wow! That's a brilliant idea!" said Shelshala. "So your dad will take the shield material to the energy plant?"

"Exactly and because the material will bond and expand, only a tiny amount will need to go in each bin." Henrite pointed toward a button on Shelshala's jacket. "I imagine a piece about that size should be enough for each person."

Shelshala thought through what Henrite had said. "But how is your dad going to get the material into each bin without anyone noticing?"

"Hmmm..." Henrite continued staring at the button on Shelshala's coat.

"I've got it! I've visited the plant a ton of times. The bins are put on a conveyor belt and their contents are emptied onto another conveyor belt for inspection. Then the bins continue on and are washed, dried and deodorized using a spray before being delivered back to homes.

I bet the deflector material will be added to the spray. That's it! All my dad has to do is pour it into the deodorant vat! Most likely, he'll put it in the same type of bags the deodorant comes in and have the bags delivered to the plant. I'm sure some of the deodorant company drivers will be helping out."

"High-five!" Henrite lifted his hand toward Shelshala. "I'm telling you, Shel, this is going to work! We are finally going to get rid of those numbskull guards!"

The plan sounded pretty solid. For the first time, Shelshala relaxed a little.

Now they had to get back into her mom's lab to make the final additions to the deflector material, because her mom could not risk doing it herself. The turbochargers would be a perfect excuse for them to be in the lab, but they still needed to be very careful. They couldn't have something go wrong now!

The friends memorized the ingredients in Henrite's dad's note and tore the note into tiny, tiny pieces. Henrite put them into his jacket pocket to throw away when he got home.

Then they started heading out of the Shrine.

"Wait!" Shelshala cried out, grabbing Henrite's arm. "Now that it's officially on, we need to give our plan a name!"

"Totally! How about Mission Kakamuchu-Sucks?" suggested Henrite.

"That will make everyone take us real seriously."

"How 'bout Mission Guards-Out."

"Good," said Shelshala, "but might be a little confusing. How about something about laughter? It is the No-Laughter decree that started it all."

"Laughter...laughing," Henrite thought out loud as he balanced back and forth on his wheels. "Got it! 'Laughing-Rules Day'."

"What about Laugh-Out-Loud Day?" asked Shelshala. "That's what we're gonna be asking everyone to do."

Henrite stopped rocking. "I like it! Mission Laugh-Out-Loud is ready for launch! Kakamuchu, the battle is on!" He karate chopped an imaginary Kakamuchu in the air.

They would meet at Shelshala's house to add the rest of the ingredients to the shield the next day.

28

FINISHING THE DEFLECTOR

Tomorrow took forever and once again Henrite and Shelshala barely paid attention to a word their teachers said. The day had never been so long! When they finally were dismissed, it took all their self-control not to put their wheels in highest gear to get to Shelshala's house, guards or no guards.

When they got there, Shelshala's mom was sitting on the couch in the living room reading. Her dad wasn't home yet.

"Hi, Mom."

"Hi, Dr. K."

"Hey, kids. How was school?"

Shelshala and Henrite both frowned.

Dr. Kakachala smiled. "Say no more. So, what are you up to?"

Shelshala asked, "Is it okay for us to work on our turbochargers in your lab?"

"Sure, I've already left the chargers there for you," her mom said. "Just make sure you don't touch anything you aren't familiar with. Come and ask me questions before trying anything out on your own."

"Thanks Mom, we'll be careful."

"Thanks Dr. K."

The kids grabbed a bowl of tangoberries (berries with a tangy sweet taste a lot like candy) from the kitchen counter and headed for the lab.

Once in the lab, in case anyone was spying through the Crysquid, they needed to make it look as if they were working on the chargers lying on one of the tables.

They sat down at the table.

"So these are the basic chargers. We need to figure out how to modify them to go faster," said Henrite.

"Yeah, remember our class about thermodynamics?" asked Shelshala.

"Sorta. I generally start fading after history," said Henrite.

"I'd say you start fading the minute you get to school."

"Ha ha. What about thermodynamics?"

"That's what we'll need to study to figure out how to go faster—but not too fast, or we'll lose control around the curves. Shelshala turned on the lab tablet propped up on the table and did a search for 'thermodynamic basics'.

"We need to start with this," Shelshala pointed at a book chapter that had opened on the tablet.

Henrite took a quick look at the tablet screen, got up from the stool he was sitting on and wheeled around the lab. "I still can't believe all the cool stuff your mom has in here. I think I want to be a scientist or inventor. Look at this stuff. I wonder what it's for." He pulled down one of the chemicals they needed off a shelf. It was clear with sparkling speckles throughout.

"Be careful! My mom already noticed some of her chemicals were missing from the last time we were playing around in here!"

"No way! You didn't tell me."

Henrite turned toward the place they had hid the shield material the last time they were in the lab. "Hey, that reminds me, let's add some more stuff to that plasticy thing we made last time. Maybe it'll turn into something cool."

"Are you kidding? My mom could walk in any minute!"

"Ahh, don't be a wimp. The door's open. We'll hear her if she's coming."

Shelshala glanced at the door. "Okay. But, hurry up! She'll go ballistic if she catches us playing around in here."

She was going along with Henrite about just happening to remember the shield substance they had made before. They didn't want to leave a doubt in the mind of anyone who might be watching through the Crysquid that they were just two kids messing around where they weren't supposed to.

Henrite went behind the container where they had hid the shield substance and brought the substance to the table.

They added all the ingredients they had memorized from the list in Henrite's dad's note. About an hour later, just as they were finishing up, they heard Shelshala's mom wheeling toward the lab.

"Hurry, put it back! She's coming!" Shelshala whispered.

"Drats, it doesn't look any different!" Henrite complained, as he put the substance back behind the container.

He was just sitting back down at the table when Dr. Kakachala wheeled into the lab.

29

SHELSHALA'S MOM HAS IT UNDER CONTROL

The kids acted as if they were examining the turbochargers.

"How's it going?" Shelshala's mom asked.

Henrite gave her a thumbs-up, letting her know they had added the additional ingredients to the deflector material. "Lookin' good, Dr. K!"

"Oh Mom, can't you just tell us what to do to make the turbocharging stronger? Thermodynamics are boring," complained Shelshala.

"If you want a chance at winning the race, you'd better start thinking thermodynamics are very interesting," her mom replied. "Get back to reading! I'll check on you again in a bit."

As she started to leave the lab, she glanced at the container the shield material was hidden behind. "That's weird. That container of Nitromethane looks like it's been moved. You guys didn't touch it, did you? Nitromethane is highly flammable!"

Shelshala and Henrite did not have a clue what she was doing, so they didn't say anything.

She walked to the container, looked around it, and found the shield material.

"WHAT'S THIS! Have you guys been playing around in here? How many times have I told you a laboratory is not a playground! Never mind, don't answer. Finish up what you were supposed to be doing and we will talk about this later. I have to make sure this stuff is not harmful before getting rid of it!"

She glared at them and left the lab with the shield material in her hands. Shelshala and Henrite turned back to the chapter on thermodynamics.

About halfway through Dr. Kakachala's lecture, they had figured out what was going on. She couldn't just go behind the container and pick up the shield material when she was in the lab by herself. If the guards didn't remember that the kids had been 'fooling around', they might think she'd made it and question her. Now Shelshala's mom had made it clear she had nothing to do with the substance and that she was planning on throwing it away. Very smart thinking!

The kids continued to play-act for the Crysquid.

"She sounded really mad!" said Henrite.

"Yeah, I doubt she'll let us be in the lab by ourselves anymore. We'd better start reading. At least we'll have done what we were supposed to."

They stayed in the lab for another half hour, reading about thermodynamic principles. When they left the lab, Shelshala's mom was setting the table for dinner.

"Hopefully you guys actually will have some theories to test and aren't going to be begging me to help you at the last minute," she said jokingly.

"We will! And, sorry Mom, for messing around," said Shelshala.

"Yeah, real sorry Dr. K," said Henrite.

"It's late now. But we will be having a talk about your irresponsible behavior. Thank goodness the material you guys put together was inert. Really, what were you thinking?"

"Sorry Mom, it won't happen again," promised Shelshala.

"It better not," warned her mom. "Bye Henrite. Say hi to your mom and dad for me."

"Will do," Henrite said as he headed toward the door. "See ya tomorrow, Shel."

Mission accomplished—and what a great acting job by all!

30

CREATING THE MESSAGE

MORE WAITING. Shelshala and Henrite still hadn't heard from their parents about what day should be designated as Laugh-Out-Loud Day, so they could create the message for Kenakada to stream on the Crysquid.

Also, what was up with Kenakada? Not a peep out of him! How could he know what was going on and not even try to find out how things were going? Shelshala decided he must be a freak of nature. Sometimes she felt like pinching him when she passed his desk, just to make sure he was actually alive.

Two weeks passed and then, one morning when Henrite got to school, he had a grin on his face about as wide as a mozzlie (a Kakalilian banana). He obviously had some news. But—ARGH!—Shelshala would have to wait until after school to find out.

Kenakada must have been paying more attention than she thought. He must have noticed how excited Henrite was because during math class she received a message from him on her tablet. It was a simple '?'. She responded with 'Very Soon!'.

Somehow Shelshala and Henrite made it through the school day and headed to the wilderness. Once at the Shrine, Henrite took out the note. He hadn't read it yet either.

*Get your team together on the 5th of Augiter
to discuss the details of the race. Looks like
everything should be ready for a run on the following
day, the 6th. - Dad*

"Four days from now? That doesn't give us much time!" said Henrite.

"We need to let Kenakada know!" said Shelshala.

"Yeah. But let's put together the message first, so we can give it to him when we meet up."

"Good idea. The fewer meetings, the better. Let's work on what we're going to say in the message now and record it tomorrow. We can meet with Kenakada the day after that."

"The message…Should we be the ones saying it?" asked Henrite. "I mean, will anyone believe us, being kids and all?"

"It looks like our parents think we should do it," said Shelshala. "Just because we're kids doesn't mean we can't think!"

"You're right," said Henrite. "I guess it doesn't really matter who makes the announcement. It just matters who wants to believe it."

"Or isn't too scared to participate," added Shelshala.

In all the excitement of planning, they really hadn't given much thought to the fact that all the work and organizing they had done meant nothing if the Kakalilians wouldn't help. The plan's success definitely required a team effort.

A shadow of doubt crossed Shelshala's face. "What if not enough people show up? There will still be guards left… Oh no, what if we get even more people vanished?"

Even though he had no idea what was going to happen, Henrite wasn't going to let Shelshala freak out about all the things that could go wrong. "Are you kidding me? Every single one of them is going to show, because we're going to convince them! After our knock-out message, everybody's going to be so pumped to get rid of the stinkin' guards!"

Shelshala smiled at his enthusiasm. Henrite was right. They had gotten this far. All their work wasn't going to be for nothing. "You're right! It's all about the message. It's gotta be perfect. We've just got to figure out what to say!"

It didn't take them long to put something together. They had both been thinking about the message for a long time.

They soon came up with an outline for the announcement they would record the next day:

1- Introduce ourselves.

2- Explain how hard it is to be a kid on Kaka-La. How it seems like every day there is one more thing we aren't allowed to do. How the No-Laughter decree takes all the fun out of being a kid.

3- Describe the Laugh-Out-Loud mission and how our parents helped us organize all the details. Assure the viewers that Shelshala's mom is 98.25% sure the deflectors will work.

4- Explain what everyone needs to do for the plan to work.

5- Encourage everyone to believe in the plan. Talk about their concerns and make them understand that it will not work without their participation.

6- Remind everyone that they need to put the deflector shields on the next day and come outdoors at 13:30pm, half an hour after noon (14 o'clock)*.

7- The message must not be longer than 4 minutes and 40 seconds.

Two days later, they met with Kenakada and gave him the message they had recorded on a data storage button.

"Will this work for you?" asked Henrite.

"Yep. I'll load it on my tablet."

"And are you still sure you can transmit? Otherwise, nothing will work," said Shelshala.

"Chill. Everything is set. Nothing is going to go wrong with the message."

Shelshala gave out a loud sigh. "Sorry, I'm just really nervous."

"No worries. I get it. So, about an hour and a half after dusk, right?" said Kenakada.

"Yeah. Everyone should be home by then," said Henrite.

"Okay then, we're good. Should we head out?"

"Sure," said Henrite.

They left the cave together. Shelshala thought it was great that Kenakada was so confident, but it didn't do a thing to help calm the butterflies in her stomach.

---

* On Kaka-La a solar day (one rotation compared to the sun in their galaxy) is 28 hours instead of 24 hours as on Earth. Clocks start at 28 at the top and clock hands move in a counterclockwise direction (opposite of Earth clocks), counting down the hours remaining in the day until 1 o'clock (one hour left in the day). So, 22 o'clock means there are 22 hours left in the day and 6:30 means there are 6 and one half hours left in the day.

31

THE POINT OF NO RETURN

The next day, Shelshala and Henrite went to school as usual. Both had tossed and turned all night in their sleep and were exhausted. Even calming mist had not helped their nerves.

In science class, when Mrs. Jamalku asked, "What is the difference between fission and fusion?" Shelshala, who had dozed off, mumbled, "In a second, Mom. Let me sleep a little longer." She woke up with a start as Mrs. Jamalku blew her horn to prevent anyone from laughing. Shelshala turned bright green. Mrs. Jamalku gave her an outdoor pass and suggested that she take a quick walk to get some fresh air.

Henrite had so much nervous energy that his leg kept shaking under his desk. He was too tired to notice the rattling sound his wheels were making until Mr. Makulaka, their math teacher, stopped his lesson.

"Class, do you hear that rattling?"

All eyes turned to Henrite.

At first, Henrite wondered why everyone was looking at him. The he realized he was the one responsible for the rattling!

"Oops, sorry about that," he said sheepishly as he stopped shaking his leg.

Of course, Kenakada was as cool as a jalamakata (a Kakalilian cucumber). He was the one with the greatest responsibility on that day, but looked as if he didn't have a care in the world. Shelshala went between thinking he was the most irritating person on Kaka-La to thinking he was the most amazing. Someone needed to do a scientific study on him to see if he had ice in his blood or something. For Shelshala, who was always reacting to everything, it was just beyond belief that someone could be so mellow.

That evening, Henrite and his family came over to Shelshala's house so that the kids could watch the Crysquid transmission together. Shelshala and Henrite tried to fight the urge to keep checking the Crysquid as it got closer to the time for transmission. Shelshala's dad finally gave her a warning glance after the third or fourth time he'd caught her looking at it. After that, she kept her head down and didn't look up at all.

About an hour and a half after dusk, the Crysquid screen started flickering and crackling. Shelshala and Henrite both jumped up from where they were sitting on the couch. Their parents also slowly got up from where they were sitting. Henrite jumped up so quickly, he knocked his knee into the table. Shelshala turned as pale as a ghost, with her heart racing a mile a minute. Then, for a few seconds, the screen went black again. Shelshala turned to her mom with a look of despair. Henrite couldn't ignore the pain in his leg anymore and bent down to rub it, but didn't take his eyes off the screen for a second. Just as Shelshala was about to burst from the stress that had been building up inside her all day, the screen flickered again and revealed her and Henrite's video. Kenakada had done it! He had made it happen! Shelshala quickly threw a wide smile at Henrite and turned her attention back to the screen, her hands clasped at her chest. Henrite stood up and stared at the screen even though his leg was still throbbing badly.

Kakalilians everywhere heard the following message in their homes.

SHELSHALA: "Hi everyone, I'm Shelshala Kakachala."

HENRITE: "And I'm Henrite Kalamayo."

SHELSHALA: "We have put together a quick message for you. Please do not be concerned about it being detected. Our friend Kenakada Pentoma has intercepted the Crysquid feed into your homes. The guards are unaware of the interception.

It has become unbearable being a kid on Kaka-La. We know that we are supposed to be patient and understanding about our leader Kakamuchu's decrees, but they have just become too mean. First, we had to stay in school all day without recess and then we weren't supposed to eat sweets or make too much noise when we played outside. Now, with the horrible No-Laughter decree, our parents won't allow us to do anything fun that might make us laugh. We just can't live like this anymore!

And even more importantly, thousands of our people have been vanished by the Royal Guards. These are our family members, friends and neighbors. We miss them and hope that wherever they are, they are alive and well. But, if they are somewhere that does not have the right conditions for survival, we must locate and save them before their hibernation state comes to an end. We want to bring them back to Kaka-La where they belong!

HENRITE: We have developed a plan to get rid of the Royal Guards.

We will vanish them like they have been vanishing us. We have created a shield that will deflect Vanisher rays. So, when guards shoot at someone, the ray will rebound off the shield and hit them. Once all the guards are vanished, we will find out from Kakamuchu where everyone has been vanished to and bring them home!

Our parents have helped us create the shield and organize all the details of the plan. Shelshala's mom, Dr. Kakachala has calculated a 98.25% guarantee that the deflector shields will work.

SHELSHALA: In order for our plan to work, all the guards have to be vanished at the same time, or else we will be put under house arrest until more guards are brought from Doofusturn. Our plan will not work without your help.

Tomorrow morning you will find a small ball of transparent deflector material in your energy recycle bin. Tear it into enough pieces for all the members of your family. Give everyone a piece. Rub the material between your hands like this—

On the screen, Shelshala rubbed the palm of her hands together to show the viewers what to do.

You will feel a tingle in your hands as the shield material bonds with your skin and spreads all over you body. It will take less than a minute for the shield to cover you from head to toe. Continue your day as normal until 13:30 PM. At exactly 13:30PM, please stop whatever you are doing, go outdoors and start laughing. You will be protected by the shield, which will deflect the rays. When the guards start shooting, they will vanish themselves. Kaka-La will become guard free!

HENRITE: We understand that our plan is coming out of nowhere and you have every right to be concerned about how well it will work. If there was more time or a way we could talk with each of you about the planning that has gone into it, we would! But, as you know, there is no way we can without the guards becoming suspicious. So, we are asking you to trust us and join us in freeing Kaka-La!

SHELSHALA: Yes, we are kids, but we are kids who care about our family and friends and the future of Kaka-La. We dream about Kaka-La being a happy place again. Please help us make this dream come true. Remember to put your shields on tomorrow and join us at 13:30PM to bring an end to the rule of the guards! Complete secrecy is absolutely necessary! Please go about your days as normal. Anything out of the ordinary could alert the guards. If a word of our plan leaks, it is done for. We have this one chance! Please join us. We believe in you! Please believe in us and the possibility of freedom! Let's bring the Vanished home!!!

The Crysquid screen went black.

Henrite and Shelshala turned towards each other and double high fived. They did it!!! The message was out!!! Their parents, who had heard the message for the first time, came over to give them both big hugs. They couldn't risk talking about the message because the Crysquid might have already reverted back to normal mode. Shelshala's dad, who up to this point had reluctantly gone along with the plan, whispered in Shelshala's ear: "You are a mighty brave girl. I am so proud of you!"

Once back at his house, the only way Henrite could release his nervous energy was to wheel up and down all the ramps in the house.

There was little sleeping in either house that night except for Candicala who had no clue what was going on.

In fact, there were very few Kakalilians who fell asleep that night. With the exception of Kenakada, of course — he slept like a baby. As far as he was concerned the game was on and he was ready for some major Royal Guard and Kakamuchu butt-kicking!

32

MISSION LAUGH-OUT-LOUD

The next day, every household in Kaka-La found a ball of transparent shield material in their recycling bin. The shields attached to the body exactly as Shelshala had described in the message, with a tingling sensation spreading throughout the body as the shield covered the wearer from head to toe. After Shelshala and Henrite put their shields on, they said goodbye to their families and met each other at their front gates. They started on their way to school in silence.

Both were still very emotional from the goodbyes that had taken place in their houses. With the ever-present Crysquid, everyone had to act as normal as possible as they got ready to leave the house. Life had to go on as usual. That meant that when the Laugh-Out-Loud moment happened, most families would not be together. If the plan didn't work, some of them might not see each other again.

Henrite's mom had a really hard time keeping it together. Finally, when she could no longer hold back her tears, she acted as if something had gotten into her eye and rushed to the bathroom.

The kids were about halfway to school when Henrite ended the silence.

"So, how ya doin'?" he asked quietly.

With a weak smile, Shelshala said, "Hanging in there. It's the not knowing what's going to happen that's driving me crazy."

"I know the feeling."

Up to this point, they had been so distracted by their own thoughts they hadn't really been paying attention to anyone around them. But now they began to notice quick glances and smiles from the people passing by them. They had recognized them from the message and were letting Shelshala and Henrite know that they were on board with the plan.

Henrite and Shelshala went from utter surprise and anxiety to hopefulness again. This was the first time they had got a real response to their plan. It was no longer only in their heads. It has a life of its own!

But just as the encouraging glances began to lift their spirits, they noticed other people who passed right by them without making eye contact, or, possibly, deliberately avoiding them.

Shelshala anxiously glanced over at Henrite. They were both thinking the same thing.

What did that mean? Were they mad at them? Were they letting them know they weren't going to participate in the plan? What if not enough Kakalilians showed up?

Shelshala quickly said, "You count plus. I'll count minus."

Henrite nodded. For the rest of the way to school, he tried to count all the smiles, while Shelshala counted the no-eye-contacts.

As they reached the school gates, Shelshala said, "82."

"85," said Henrite.

Shelshala's shoulders slumped. "Oh no! What does that mean?"

"It's okay, Shel. We don't know what it means. We're just going to have to wait and see." He was not feeling so great himself, but didn't want to make Shelshala more worried than she already was — if that were even possible.

As they entered the schoolyard, all eyes were on them. They quickly wheeled to their classroom to avoid the attention. What if the guards noticed something was going on?

Kenakada was already in his seat, looking totally unfazed. He had gotten to school early to avoid contact with anyone.

He greeted Shelshala and Henrite with a "Hey" and a nod of his head and then turned back to his tablet.

It took Henrite and Shelshala a few minutes to regain their composure. She took out her tablet and acted as if she were reading something on it, while he fiddled with his. Shelshala was actually feeling kind of faint from nerves.

As the bell rang and other kids straggled into class, Shelshala and Henrite kept their heads down and pretended to be busy. They could feel a kind of nervous energy flowing through the classroom that was very different from that of a usual uneventful morning. Shelshala was very concerned. What if everywhere was like their classroom? Would the guards notice that something was up? There were still a few hours left until the Laugh-Out-Loud moment.

She had never been happier to see Mr. Makulaka. She could have kissed him as he started their math lesson as usual without even glancing Shelshala, Henrite, or Kenakada's way.

The morning hours passed miserably slow. There wasn't a peep from anyone, except to answer teachers' questions, generally with wrong answers. Shelshala caught Henrite's eye a few times. She could tell it was taking all his willpower to stay quiet. Quiet was not something he did well in normal circumstances, let alone this. She wasn't doing so well herself. The knot in her stomach that had formed as she counted the 'no-eye-contacts' had only gotten tighter. And, her mom had made her wear her hair in a ponytail after the last round of Hair Growth cream, so she didn't have anything to chew on to relieve her stress.

Math.

History.

Science. This was it!

12:30, 12:33, 12:35, 12:39...

13:01, 13:03, 13:07...

13:27, 13:28, 13:29...

33

L A U G H   O U T   L O U D ! ! !

13:30.

Mrs. Jamalku stopped her lesson. "I am going to step out awhile. You can stay in class or take a break if you like." She left the classroom without another word.

At first, the kids in the classroom seemed unsure what to do. Kenakada was the first to get up and head out the door. Henrite and Shelshala followed. They heard the sound of chairs being pulled back behind them as more kids got up. In the hallway, kids and adults were coming out of classrooms and down the ramps from the second floor, all moving in the direction of the main entrance. Some kids were holding hands, others anxiously looked around them, while still others shared nervous smiles. It was pretty quiet except for the sound of wheels rolling down the hallway.

Once outside, most kids moved toward teachers they knew. As the group outside got larger, guards started gathering above them.

"Go back to your classes immediately!" they cried through their blastocoms. Everyone stood their ground. It took about another ten minutes for everybody to find their way out of the building. No one was sure what would happen next.

A rush of faces turned toward Shelshala and Henrite who were confused at first before realizing that everyone must be waiting for them to lead the Laugh-Out-Loud moment. Kids and teachers started to form a wide semi-circle around them.

As guards landed their motokalins, Henrite tried to laugh. He was so nervous that the sound came out more like a cough. He frantically turned to Shelshala; he couldn't make himself laugh! For a second, Shelshala felt a rush of panic. They hadn't thought of this part. How do you make yourself laugh, especially when you're terrified?

A light bulb went on in Shelshala's head. She knew exactly what to do. She turned and started tickling Henrite.

Henrite jumped up. He let out a "Hey!"

She kept on tickling him and he started laughing for real. She giggled at the sight of him jumping around trying to avoid being tickled. It felt awesome to finally laugh.

Everyone stared in disbelief as one of the guards who had landed aimed his Vanisher at Henrite and Shelshala. The two looked straight at the guard, laughing in his face. Without a second's thought, the guard pulled the trigger.

A collective gasp rose from the crowd as a blue laser beam sped in Henrite and Shelshala's direction. The gasp turned to cries of astonishment as Kenakada, who was standing beside Henrite, threw himself in the path of the laser beam. As the beam struck him, his whole body quivered. The deflector shield covering his body turned neon blue as it absorbed the full force of the laser. And then, the blue tint contracted back to the center of his body and shot back out toward the guard, hitting him straight in the leg.

The guard vanished into thin air.

In shock from what had just occurred in front of their eyes, the crowd was silent. By this time, all the guards had landed and were pointing their Vanishers across the schoolyard.

At first, the sound of forced giggles could be heard here and there. Then, one of the boys towards the front of the semi-circle kicked a friend in the butt. His friend flew forward and yelled out, "Hey, what the—"

Those standing around them broke out in spontaneous laughter. Other kids started tickling each other. Another group formed a chain and wheeled around the schoolyard at top speed. As the crowd became rowdier, the not so bright guards, as expected, started shooting randomly. With every shot a quiver went through the intended victim as the shield absorbed the beam and then aimed it right back at the shooter. Neon blue spots flashed across the crowds as each guard became the target of a deflected beam.

Minutes passed like seconds.

Then a voice rose above the chaos. "They're gone! They're gone! The guards have all disappeared!"

It took awhile for news of the guards' vanishing to spread across the astonished crowd. People started hugging, high-fiving, wheeling and jumping around. Some kids hopped on the vanished guards' motokalins and flew up into the air. They had no idea how to control the machines. Some figured how to operate the vehicles pretty quickly, while others were totally out of control, diving into the crowd and back up again. Other riders yelled directions to them while teachers on the ground yelled, "Get down! Land the machines before you get hurt!"

The group closest to Shelshala and Henrite started chanting, "Henrite and Shelshala!" The two found themselves lifted above the group and carried on shoulders.

"Wait!" yelled Shelshala above the cheers. "Kenakada...don't forget Kenakada!"

Kenakada still felt a little dazed from the force of the laser beam hitting his body. A few hands hoisted him up.

The group made its way out of the schoolyard and toward the city center. Some kids and adults continued celebrating in the schoolyard, while others headed home to find loved ones.

Sitting atop the group of excited kids, Shelshala, Henrite and Kenakada had a view of the celebrations happening throughout the streets.

Henrite pumped his fist in the air, yelling excitedly: "There's not a guard in sight!"

Shelshala nodded her head in agreement as she beamed with pleasure. She was far too excited to speak.

As the Kakalilians had poured onto the streets, the guards went into high alert. Those working in the Ministry of Homeland Tranquility buildings throughout the city joined the guards patrolling the street to smash the uprising. And, as predicted, once the guards started shooting, they did not stop until they had all vanished themselves.

As Shelshala, Henrite and Kenakada were carried along in the rush of jubilant celebrations, they could make out cries of "Thanks!", "Congratulations!" and "We love you!" directed their way.

The city overflowed with happiness. Florists handed out bunches of flowers, which were immediately thrown into the air, turning the sky into a kaleidoscope of vibrant colors. Music could be heard through the doors and windows of some buildings as people danced in the streets; apparently the guards hadn't confiscated ALL the music files. Confetti covered the ground. People carriers honked their horns in the sky, as elderly Kakalilian passengers joyfully cried out through the windows. Every Kakalilian throughout the land laughed with joy. Even babies gurgled with pleasure in their carriages.

As the crowds grew bigger, it became impossible for the group of kids to stay together. Shelshala, Henrite, and Kenakada came down onto the ground and found themselves swept away in the festivities.

Someone grabbed Shelshala and started twirling her around.

"Grab my hand!" yelled Henrite.

As she twirled, she managed to grab hold of Henrite's hand and he pulled her toward him. They inched their way out of the city square and leaned against a building to catch their breath.

Kenakada was standing a little to their left. "What took you guys so long?"

Still a little out of breath, Henrite asked, "How'd you get here so fast?"

"Sometimes the way you act, I think you're from another planet!" added Shelshala.

"Well I'm not. And, in case you guys forgot, this whole thing was about Kakamuchu and finding the Vanished." Kenakada tilted his head up toward Mount KalaKala. "I believe he's still living it up in his digs."

"Kakamuchu!" said Henrite. "We hadn't thought that far ahead when we were planning! Whaddaya think we should do about him? Should we head to the castle now? Or, find our parents first?"

Without hesitation Kenakada said, "No way, man. We can't wait. He might get away! The guards are gone. He has no one left to hide his sorry self behind."

Shelshala agreed. "Maybe he doesn't know what's happened yet. We've got to risk it and go up there. He's the only one who can tell us where the Vanished are. I doubt anyone else is thinking about him right now."

"You're not getting any argument from me! But, how are we going to get through THAT?" said Henrite, looking at the celebrations in full force as far as the eye could see.

"No problem, man. We're golden." Kenakada glanced over at three unattended motokalins a few feet away from them.

They hopped on the motokalins. Kenakada gave them quick instructions on how they operated. Shelshala and Henrite did not even bother to ask him how he knew. He was Kenakada. No more needed to be said.

They took off into the sky and headed up toward the castle.

34

KAKAMUCHU APPEARS

As they flew toward the castle, the boys started messing around on the motokalins, racing each other and doing aerial wheelies. Shelshala put a quick stop to their antics with a killer glare that made them both line up beside her sheepishly.

When they reached the castle, they landed a few feet in front of the gate. The castle was eerily quiet; no one was in sight. It was hard to believe there were wild and exuberant celebrations in the valley below.

As they walked toward the gate, Henrite whispered, "Do you think there are some more guards inside?"

"I'm not sure," said Shelshala. "It looks pretty empty. I think they would have come out by now if they saw us landing."

"Yeah, most likely they all headed into the city," said Kenakada.

"Well, we're about to find out." Henrite pushed against the amber crystal palace gate doors towering above them. They didn't budge. Then, as if Henrite's touch had triggered a switch, the doors started to open toward them. The kids wheeled quickly back out of the way.

As they were moving, the open gates revealed four guards wielding Vanishers. They started shooting.

"Curl up!" yelled Kenakada.

He didn't know for sure if curling up would help, but after getting hit with a laser in the school yard, he thought that not taking a wide open shot to the body might lessen the impact.

The beams hit them and then rebounded back at the guards.

Curling up had helped with the impact. The kids felt sore, but nowhere near as disoriented as Kenakada had felt when he was hit before. The guards vanished and the kids readied themselves for more guards to come.

None did. They had just vanished the last of Kaka-muchu's Elite Palace Guards. The rest had gone to the city when the high alert was activated. Kaka-La was guard free!!!

35

SO NOW HE'S MISTER NICE GUY

From a peephole in the curtains in his secluded third floor sitting room, Kakamuchu saw the guards vanishing. He almost immediately knew what the Kakalilians had accomplished. After all, he had invented the Vanisher and was aware it was possible to create a deflector. He just did not understand how it had been done when guards were always watching the activities of the scientists, engineers and inventors.

Who had done this? And what did they want? He knew the Kakalilians were naturally a peace-loving people. They had never fought back before. Why were they fighting back now?

He decided he would go out and meet the children to learn more before he made his next move. He was already formulating a plan.

He stepped onto a balcony facing the children. He was dressed in black from head to toe. A tall crown decorated with jet black crystals glittered on his head and a velvet cape covered with the same crystals was draped around his shoulders.

"My young Kakalilian friends, it is I, your ruler. Welcome!" said Kakamuchu with a theatrical wave of his arm. Black gloves embellished with dark purple crystals covered his hands, the only touch of color visible on his body.

"A million thanks for ridding us of the evil guards! They have been holding me captive and making me sign horrible decrees. We are all now liberated from their tyranny! Kaka-La is free again!"

The kids were not at all fooled by Kakamuchu's claim that the guards had controlled him. Henrite let out a "Ha", but it was not loud enough to reach Kakamuchu.

Shelshala whispered, "Shhh! Let him talk. We're not going to get the info we need if he thinks we don't believe him."

Kakamuchu continued his speech, placing his gloved hands on the balcony balustrade and dramatically leaning out toward the children.

"When the evil guards first came to our planet from Doofusturn they planned on getting rid of all the citizens of Kaka-La so they could settle their own people here. I convinced them they would have more power if they stayed here and ruled over us, rather than bringing more of their own kind. I was very convincing and, finally, they agreed not to go back to their planet to bring more warriors. I saved you all. But only under the condition that the guards be permitted to rule as they wish.

"My friends, I had no choice." Kakamuchu let out a deep sigh and raised a hand to his forehead, as if to express great distress. "I was as much a victim of their evil acts as you. Now you have saved me! An infinity of thanks. Who among my dear Kakalilians is responsible for saving us? Who came up with the brilliant plan? I want to meet and reward them."

Shelshala moved a few steps closer to the balcony, took a deep breath and raised her voice. "We all worked together to stop the evil guards, Mega Uber Majesty. We are very happy to hear we saved you from them as well. Now we are in need of your superior intelligence." She knew he would respond to flattery.

"Could you help us find the Vanished? We know the ray guns shattered them into millions of pieces. But we believe their pieces must come back together again somewhere in the galaxy."

"Dear child, what is your name?" said Kakamuchu.

"My name is Shelshala and these are my friends, Henrite and Kenakada. "

"Dear children, of course I will help you. They are my loved ones as well. Oh, how I have suffered to think of them somewhere out of our reach. Come into the castle and we will find out how to save them together. Then, this evening, I will throw a liberation celebration party at the castle for all your friends and family to attend!"

"Thank you, Your Mega Uber Majesty. We would love to see inside your castle!"

"Excellent. I will open the doors and meet you downstairs."

The kids looked at one another as the ornate steel castle doors opened to their right. They knew they were going into a dangerous situation. Kakamuchu was very smart and devious. If they waited for adults to arrive, he would surely escape. Then they would never know where the Vanished were.

So they headed into the castle.

36

INSIDE THE FORBIDDEN CASTLE

The castle was dark. The kids found themselves in a very large circular entry hall. The curtains were drawn on six windows that rose from floor to ceiling on each side of the room. A magnificent chandelier of black crystals hanging from the domed ceiling was the only source of light. Portraits of previous Supreme Rulers of Kaka-La hung on the walls between the windows.

Directly in front of the kids, a wide ramp extended across the back of the hall and sloped upward to the castle's second floor. At the top of the ramp, in front of a gigantic image of his profile created with crystals, stood Kakamuchu.

"He sure likes crystals!" whispered Henrite. Shelshala and Kenakada nervously chuckled in response.

"Welcome, welcome," Kakamuchu said with his arms extended. The kids had only seen him from afar when he sat in his Kaka-luto. They had no idea he was so tall and pale from spending most of his time indoors. He had taken off his crown, cape and gloves. His hands and feet glittered brightly as he wheeled down the ramp. The curtains covering the windows automatically rose as he moved toward them. Sunshine poured into the room and hit the crystal chandelier. The reflection of the sun off the crystals was almost blindingly bright. The kids shielded their eyes with their arms.

Kakamuchu landed at the bottom of the ramp and wheeled toward them at top speed. Still shielding their eyes, the kids sensed more than saw how quickly he was moving. They gave a collective gasp, expecting him to run right into them. Instead, he came to a complete stop on his front wheel only steps in front of Shelshala. Henrite and Kenakada looked at each other in amazement, both thinking: "How'd he do that???" They really did not want to admire his wheeling skills, but they could not help but be impressed.

"Oh dear! The light is bothering you. Sincere apologies. I have protective shields on my eyes. Nothing can harm my sight. Of course, you poor things only have basic optic functions. How thoughtless of me!" With a wave of his hand, the curtains started to come down. "There you are. That should be better."

The kids lowered their arms and looked full on at Kakamuchu's face. In contrast to his paleness, his eyes were the most incredible shade of purple speckled with gold. They had never seen purple eyes before, let alone with gold speckles. They could now make out that his hands were covered with crystals in elaborate geometric designs that appeared to continue up his arms. They couldn't tell for sure because his shirt was long-sleeved. His wheels were also covered with black crystals. He was quite a spectacular figure. The kids could not help but feel a little awed and intimidated.

Kakamuchu was fully aware of the effect he had on people when they first met him. He injected his eyes with a special dye he had created many years ago. They could be any color he desired. Before coming down to meet the children, he had injected the purple because he knew it was particularly spectacular. And the crystal designs on his hands and arms had taken a crystal tattoo artist months to create to his liking. He intended to use his outstanding appearance to

his full advantage in order to get what he needed from these kids.

As he gave them a wide smile oozing with deception, they saw that his teeth were also covered in clear crystals that glittered when he talked.

"So happy you came! It has been so long since I have had visitors. The guards forbade it. I have so much to show you. I do not know where to begin! Let me think." He stroked his chin as if he were thinking, when in fact he already knew where he intended on taking the children.

"I got it! Of course, the laboratory! What was I thinking? That is where we will start. You will love it. Quite amazing! I am also confident we will find the answer to your question there. Follow me, follow me," he said as he turned around.

Kakamuchu had not extended his hand when he greeted the kids. All Kakalilians knew he did not like to be touched. But, before they entered the castle, Shelshala had already planned on doing exactly that. Kakamuchu was made of the same cellular material as they were, so she hoped the transfer of the deflector would happen if she touched him for a few seconds. They had no idea what he was up to, but at least they could make sure he had the deflector on him; anything that happened to them would then also happen to him.

"Your Mega Uber Majesty, one moment please!" she said.

Kakamuchu turned back toward them with a flash of

irritation across his face.

"Yes, dear Shelshala?"

Shelshala knelt down on her knee. "May I kiss your hand? It would mean so much to me."

For a second, Henrite and Kenakada looked at each other as if she'd lost her mind. But then they assumed she must have some reason for making such a disgusting request and followed her lead, kneeling down in front of Kakamuchu.

"Yes, Your Mega Humongous Majesty, may we kiss your hand?" said Henrite.

Kakamuchu abhorred anyone touching him. He had no memory of anyone hugging him when he was a child and as an adult, he preferred that no one get too near him. But, he needed to gain the children's trust to execute his evil plan. So, he fought his repulsion and slowly extended his hand. At least the crystals would ensure that their slimy lips not touch his skin!

"Of course, children."

On their side, the kids would rather have eaten live crataliks (Kakalilian beetles) than hold and kiss his hand. But hold and kiss they did.

Shelshala made sure to hold Kakamuchu's hand for a few seconds, touching his palm where there were no crystals.

Kakamuchu pulled his hand back as quickly as he could and turned around, reassuring himself that it would not be long before he learned what he needed. He could then disinfect his whole arm.

"Come along, children. No time to waste! We have a lot

37

KAKAMUCHU'S
AWESOME LABORATORY

Once Kakamuchu's back was to them, Henrite and
Kenakada pretended to gag and made faces of disgust.
They responded to Shelshala's warning glance with an
'ICK! You'd better have a REALLY good reason for
making us do that' look.

She ignored them and followed Kakamuchu as he
moved toward the back of the room. He stopped at a
doorway to their right. At the opening was a ramp that
spiraled downward.

The kids peeked down the ramp. There was no end in
sight. Great! Now, what should they do?

"Come, come children. Don't be afraid," said Kakamuchu.
"Where is your sense of adventure? My lab is the most
magnificent in the galaxy. Don't tell me you lack curiosity?
Why, without curiosity, you are doomed to a boring existence.
Remember, we don't have much time before preparations
for the celebrations! So are you coming are not? Off I go!"

Kakamuchu disappeared down the ramp. He knew the
children would follow. After all, Kakalilian children were
so predictable and lacking in imagination they would never
think to do anything but follow his lead!

The kids were really beginning to wonder about their decision to come into the castle. They kept reminding themselves that it was the only way they might find out where the Vanished were. Kakamuchu had said the answer would be in the lab.

"Come on, guys. We need to go. If he escapes, we've got nothing!" said Kenakada.

Shelshala and Henrite knew he was right. Who knew how long it would be before someone else showed up? So they all put their fears aside and followed Kakamuchu down the ramp.

The ramp descended a very long way. It felt as if they had been going down for about a minute at medium speed when they finally reached another opening. Once through it, they stood on a ledge overlooking a room about the size of six slimeball fields (roughly the size of four and a half Earth football fields). Kakamuchu was waiting for them.

The kids stared, their mouths agape with amazement. They had never seen such a place before. Shelshala and Henrite thought her mom's lab was cool. This place made that lab look like a kid's science kit! There was activity everywhere. Along one wall was a row of enormous digital screens, each screen showing a live video of different aquatic, terrestrial, or amphibian ecosystems across planets. On another wall were row upon row of chemicals, minerals and salts.

Across the room itself were rows of minilabs extending as far as the eye could see, each with different equipment and paraphernalia: computers, flashing lasers, tanks filled with creatures from across the galaxy, a full size rainbow.

So much activity, they could not even begin to take it all in.

Above them the ceiling was a dynamic image of their galaxy, including all the celestial bodies: planets, moons, stars, asteroids, nebulae, black holes, white holes, wormholes, meteors, comets…

As they looked up, Kakamuchu said, "Ah, yes, that is a simulation of our galaxy. It is programmed to show all celestial activities. It is possible to enter any day and time in the future or the past and see the galaxy exactly as it was or will be at that point. I think I wrote the code for that program when I was a teen. But I have something more fun to show you. Come along this way."

Kakamuchu knew there could not be much more time before adults arrived at the castle. After entering the lab with the kids, he had remotely concealed the entrance from the hallway. It was designed to blend into the wall so it could not be located. But scientists knew of the lab's existence and it would not take them long to discover a way to get in. He had little time to get the information he needed from the children.

Shelshala, Henrite and Kenakada continued looking around them in amazement as they wheeled down with Kakamuchu into the laboratory. Different types of miniature machines flew all over the lab, sometimes coming within an inch of their faces, making a full stop and then turning in another direction. The kids were startled at first, before they realized the machines would not hit them.

"Don't be frightened. They recognize matter and change course accordingly," explained Kakamuchu. "A project I completed, I believe, when I was ten."

126

About a quarter way into the lab he turned to a minilab on his right. "Here, here is what I want to show you. I know you will love it!"

They were standing in front of a long tubular structure with a door facing them.

Shelshala threw a quick glance at Henrite and Kenakada. They were all thinking the same thing: "What in the world could this be?"

38

THE X-POSURE

"This is the X-Posure. See this, this is a scanner." Kakamuchu pointed at a machine of some sort on rollers alongside the tubular structure. "When you go through the tube, this scanner creates a colored 3-D image of your skeleton, muscles, organs and blood circulation on the mirror along the inside wall of the tube.

He wheeled to the end of the tube and stopped at another machine. "When you exit, a report will be waiting for you here, describing how well your body is functioning. A checklist of health! Though who cares about the checklist? You are all young and healthy! I just want you to go through the X-Posure to experience the 3-D dynamic image of your bodies. Quite, quite fascinating!" He clasped his hands together in front of his chest and wheeled back toward them.

The kids couldn't help but be curious about the machine. They really wanted to go in, especially Kenakada who was checking out the scanner. But, of course, they were also nervous.

Almost as if he read their minds, Kakamuchu continued, "Come, we will go in together so you have no reason to be fearful!"

Shelshala and Henrite still hesitated, while Kenakada shrugged his shoulders and headed toward the structure's entrance. "Okay, after you," he said as he opened the door for Kakamuchu.

"That's the spirit, Kenakada!"

Henrite and Shelshala followed Kenakada and Kakamuchu into the tube. Shelshala was still very nervous, but assured herself that Kakamuchu couldn't do any harm when he was going in with them.

It was truly incredible! The inside of their bodies showed up as colored 3-D animations on the mirror as they moved through the tube. Henrite made faces and saw his facial muscles move. Kenakada jumped up and down and saw how his joints reacted to the impact.

The kids were having lots of fun and were kind of bummed when they reached the end of the tube. When they came out, the second machine Kakamuchu had shown them was printing something.

"Your reports," Kakamuchu explained. "But that's no fun. Just a bunch of levels of this and that: muscle strength, organ lifespan, etc. Let's just take a quick look at one and then move on to some more fun!"

Kakamuchu let the kids glance at Shelshala's report and then moved farther into the lab again.

"Let's hurry to the next station I want to share with you!"

Now, the children did not know that the X-Posure not only identified every substance inside the body, but also all the substances on a body. As Kakamuchu showed them Shelshala's report, he quickly scanned all the materials used to create the deflector and memorized them.

As they moved farther into the lab, the kids were feeling even more uneasy. But at the same time, everything was so cool.

As he led them forward, Kakamuchu moved rapidly between stations, pointing left then right then left again, talking the whole time.

"Over there, every mineral in the galaxy, over here, an aquarium with life-forms from our waters. Over here, a GPS station—I have my own satellites throughout the galaxies."

Henrite quickly picked up one of the handheld GPS devices lying on the station and put it in his pocket. The way Kakamuchu was moving, who knew where they would end up? At least the device might help someone locate them. Kenakada snuck one into his pocket, too.

Kakamuchu kept wheeling along, waving his glittering hands in the air as he talked (how he loved the sound of his own voice!). He turned a final right and passed two stations, abruptly stopping before a row of ray guns within a glass enclosure about twenty feet long and fifteen feet wide. The children almost wheeled right into him.

39

THE LASER ROOM

"Here it is: the electromagnetic spectrum station!" said Kakamuchu.

The kids were alarmed, especially Henrite and Kenakada.

"Don't be frightened. Do you still not trust me? I brought you here to see that for years I have been trying, when the guards' watchful eyes were not on me, to find a way to reverse the effects of the Vanisher. Here I have access to every wave from the electromagnetic spectrum: x-rays, y-rays, radio waves, infrared radiation, ultraviolet light, gamma rays...

"Alas, you, my people, have succeeded where I failed. You have destroyed the guards. I am so proud." Kakamuchu pretended to wipe a tear from his eye and then abruptly clapped his hands together.

"Back to business. Here is where we will work on finding out where the Vanished are. But, a little fun first! I have created a magnificent laser that will turn you every color of the rainbow. Not permanently, just for a few hours. Wouldn't it be fun if we all radiated ourselves for the party tonight? We would be walking rainbows!"

Kakamuchu did not fool the children. They knew he was up to something. But, what could it be?

Shelshala was the least concerned, because she thought Kakamuchu didn't know they had deflectors on. She was pretty sure they had transferred one to him as well. Plus, they had the GPS devices Henrite and Kenakada had picked up. They were ready for any evil plan he might have. As long as he included himself in anything he asked them to do, she was okay with following his lead.

Shelshala said, "That sounds like fun! As long as we work on locating the Vanished afterward."

Henrite and Kenakada were not at all comfortable with getting into the electromagnetic spectrum station. They gave each other 'What the heck is she doing?' glances.

"Of course, dear Shelshala, that is the main reason I brought you to this station," said Kakamuchu.

"I don't know," Henrite said doubtfully. "Maybe we could see the rest of the lab first." He was trying to buy them time in case anyone was looking for them by now.

Kenakada gave Henrite some backup. "Yeah, can't we go back and check out the aquarium? It looked really cool."

"Boys, boys, don't tell me you are going to be the naysayers and that Shelshala is the only truly adventurous one among you! Quite a shame. I will also receive a dose of the laser."

The boys turned to Shelshala. She tried to give them a look of reassurance. "Come on, guys, I really want to do this!"

They had no idea what Shelshala was thinking, but they trusted her and that was all that mattered.

"Okay then, let's do it," said Henrite with little enthusiasm.

"Great!" said Shelshala, turning back to Kakamuchu. "You are sure, Mega Uber Majesty, that no one will get hurt? Our parents will be very upset if anything happens to us." She didn't want him to think she was too eager to go in the chamber or he might become suspicious of her motives.

"Do you not trust me yet? Besides, do you think I would do anything to harm myself?"

"Of course you wouldn't!" said Shelshala. "Let's do it!"

"Excellent!" exclaimed Kakamuchu.

So the children followed Kakamuchu into the glass chamber.

"I just need to adjust the settings so that the laser beam will work on all four of us at once."

The kids stayed behind him, just to make sure he couldn't suddenly aim the laser at them.

He, in turn, was adjusting the Vanisher ray settings using the materials he had identified with the X-Posure. Now the rays would only target individuals wearing the deflector. Of course, he was completely unaware he had one on himself.

"Perfect! It's ready now. Let's all move over here in front of the gun and I will trigger it remotely."

The kids did as he directed. They each knew there was no saying what would happen next. But Shelshala felt they were taking a very well calculated risk. The odds were in their favor that, whatever evil plan Kakamuchu might have for them, it would not turn out the way he expected.

They all stood in front of the laser as Kakamuchu said, "On the count of three: close your eyes! One, two, THREE!"

40

VANISHED!

When the laser hit them, the kids felt a sharp pain shoot through their bodies. They saw each other begin to shatter into pieces and then there was emptiness... their minds shut off completely.

When they next opened their eyes, their surroundings were almost pitch black. It took them a few seconds to adjust to the darkness. They were relieved to see that their bodies were back in one piece and they were all still together. A tingling sensation lingered from the transporting; otherwise, they felt pretty normal. It was obvious that they were no longer on Kaka-La, as there was no greenery or buildings in sight; only deep craters and assorted rocks and boulders strewn on grayish clay-like dirt as far as their eyes could see.

And as Shelshala had hoped, there with them was Kakamuchu. His face was twisted in rage. No more Mr. Nice Guy!

"You imbeciles! What did you do! Why am I here with you?" As he yelled, a light bulb went on in his head. He remembered how Shelshala had insisted on kissing his hand. They had tricked him and somehow passed the deflector on to him. His eyes were raging neon purple.

"You little insects, I am going to crush you!"

As he rushed toward them threateningly, a voice rang out from behind the children.

"Do not lay a finger on the children!"

Shelshala, Henrite and Kenakada turned around as Kakamuchu stopped in his tracks. In front of them, as far as the eye could see, were rows and rows of houses made of large grey stones and scattered campfires in front of the houses. And before them stood a group of Vanished Kakalilians who had come to greet them.

"Dear children, my name is Yokanada," said the man who had stopped Kakamuchu. He slowly moved toward them. "Do not be frightened. We have all been vanished here together. It is not a beautiful place like Kaka-La. But we have, to the best of our ability, made it our home. You will be taken care of."

Kakamuchu was still seething green with rage, but stepped back away from the children. He knew he was outnumbered. Yokanada turned to him. The two men were about of equal height. Yokanada was very thin, having suffered from malnutrition, but there was something about his appearance that was quite awe inspiring.

"As for you...Kakamuchu, I believe. We, true Kakalilians, do as we were taught and not as we have been treated. No harm will come to you. You may take advantage of our shelter and food, but if you attempt to hurt anyone, you will be put under house arrest."

Kakamuchu stomped his feet and cursed aloud. But there was nothing he could do. He had been defeated at his own game!

41

WHAT A DREARY PLANET

Ignoring Kakamuchu's tantrum, Yokanada turned back to the children and hugged each of them. "Come with me. Everyone will be very happy to meet you."

Kakamuchu continued sulking, but followed a few steps behind them because he was afraid to be left alone. For all his ego and attitude, without the Royal Guards and his possessions, he was nothing more than a coward in royal clothing.

Yokanada led the children toward the group of Kakalilians waiting for them. Everyone gave them hugs. They looked at Kakamuchu with curiosity.

"Yes friends," Yokanada said, "your eyes do not deceive you—it is Kakamuchu. We will find out from the children why he is here. But first, let's take them to a warm fire."

It appeared that on this planet Yokanada was a leader of sorts. No one questioned his decision to allow Kakamuchu to roam free. They all moved to the large fire closest to them.

The kids were actually quite cold. The planet was not only dark, but very chilly. Once they started moving, it also became clear to them that the vanishing had sapped their energy.

"Sorry for the chill," said Yokanada. "The temperature only reaches a little above freezing on this planet. Come and rest. We know how weak one feels after the vanishing process."

Once seated at the fire, Henrite, Shelshala and Kenakada looked around them. They could not imagine a more depressing place. It was gray everywhere. No trees, no flowers, just a few dark puddles of liquid and a lot of rocks.

Yokanada saw the dread on their faces. He wanted to try to make them as comfortable as possible before asking them the questions that were on the minds of all those gathered around the fire.

"Yes children, this is a damaged land. It is the planet of Thereus, once a thriving place of beauty. Have you come across it in your studies?"

The children thought a moment.

"I don't remember," said Henrite.

"Me neither," added Kenakada.

"It is in a galaxy neighboring ours. Poor planet...doesn't get much attention, except from obsessed astronomers like myself."

"Now I remember!" said Shelshala. "It's the planet which all its inhabitants left because it could no longer support life."

"Very good, Shelshala! The inhabitants took and took from the planet without giving back. They, in a sense, used it all up. As to their fate, based on archeological findings

exploration teams discovered hundreds of years ago,
we assume they all left for another planet. We have not
discovered with certainty if the inhabitants found another
planet with the proper living conditions. All we know
is the destruction they left behind them.

What we have here is a planet that has for thousands of
years tried to reverse the damage done to it. It has been as
kind as it can be to us given its own struggles. Lingering
atmospheric damage created conditions that permit only
an hour or so of sunlight to reach the planet in a day. Also,
water is very limited. Only very rough and hardy vegetation
can survive. The berries that are roasting on the fire are an
example. We are lucky to have found them. The branches
from their bushes also keep our fires burning."

"Why were you vanished, Yokanada?" asked Henrite,
throwing a dirty look at Kakamuchu, who was sitting by
himself at a nearby fire.

"In my laboratory, I located this planet as the one the
Vanished were being transported to. I thought I had been
concealing my search effectively. But that was not the case.
Royal Guards were at my laboratory door only minutes
after my discovery."

"So there were Kakalilians trying to help the Vanished!"
said Shelshala.

"There were quite a few of us. Most are here now."

Yokanada paused a moment. "Forgive me, I forgot to
ask you: are you hungry?"

Even though they were, the kids had no desire to eat
the very unappetizing looking berries roasting on the fires.

Shelshala unconsciously wrinkled her noise. "Oh thank you, I am fine. I ate just before we got here." Henrite and Kenakada also turned down the shriveled berries.

Yokanada was not fooled by their claim. He smiled at their reluctance. "Then maybe you would like something to drink. I imagine you are thirsty."

"Yes, please. That would be very nice," said Shelshala.

They were handed small round bowls carved from soft wood and filled with a murky gray liquid. One was also given to Kakamuchu. They heard him mutter "Repulsive" as he drank it. They took a sip of the liquid and couldn't help the displeasure showing on their faces. It had a very bitter taste, but it was still very nice to have something to drink.

"The taste is not very pleasant, but it is boiled for safety and will keep you hydrated."

"Thank you, Yokanada," Henrite said.

Now that the kids had settled a bit and warmed themselves, Yokanada brought the conversation around to what everyone at the fireside was dying to learn.

42

THE SILLY GUARDS!

"Could you please explain to us how you ended up here with Kakamuchu?" asked Yokanada. "Perhaps you can also help us understand why, a couple of hours ago, Royal Guards started showing up."

The guards! The kids had forgotten all about the guards.

"Yokanada, where are the guards?" asked Henrite.

Yokanada chuckled softly. "When they first arrived, they were obviously very angry. Their blood pressure stabilizers seem to have collapsed in the vanishing process. They kept yelling at each other and then shooting one another with the Vanishers. Poor fools, it took them a good hour or so to realize that they would vanish each other only to reappear two minutes later! They have calmed down a bit and are sitting together around fires at the outskirt of our camp. They still yell and sometimes shoot one another. I guess they do not know what else to do with their anger!"

The kids would have loved to see the silly guards vanishing each other, but there was time for that later. More importantly, they needed to share with those around the fire what had happened on Kaka-La.

So they began their story. Word had spread across the settlement that Kakamuchu was there. As they explained what had happened, more and more people gathered around them.

When the conversation came around to Kenakada describing how he got in to the Crysquid system, a voice yelled out "Kenky? Is that you!"

Everyone turned in the direction of the voice. Someone was working his way toward the fire.

Kenakada jumped to his feet. "Ravro?"

Kenakada's cousin appeared out of the crowd.

"Yeah, man. You bet it's me!" Ravro said as he jumped forward to give Kenakada a bear hug that ended with a headlock.

"Cuz, whatcha doing here! Always copying me. No mind of your own, aye!" Even in the terrible conditions he was dealing with, Ravro still had the sense of humor that had gotten him vanished in the first place.

"What's bozo-man doing here?" Ravro asked, jerking his head in Kakamuchu's direction.

Yokanada responded, "Ravro, Kenakada and his friends were explaining this for us. Why don't you take a seat by your cousin and they can continue."

Kenakada was beaming with happiness. Henrite and Shelshala had never seen him so excited about anything.

Once Ravro sat, things quieted down and the kids continued their story.

It took over an hour to explain everything to Yokanada and the other Kakalilians gathered around the fire.

At the end of their story, Henrite and Kenakada pulled the GPS devices out of their pockets.

"Here they are," said Henrite. "If they are working, as soon as someone gets into the palace lab, they should be able to locate us."

Word spread across the different fireside conversations of a possible rescue. A buzz of excitement was alive in the air. Could it be true that they would be saved? Was it possible that they would get to see their loved ones and Kaka-La again?

"How amazingly clever, children. I am so proud of you!" said Yokanada. "May I take the trackers? We can check and see if they are functioning. And, if not, we might be able to activate them."

Yokanada handed the devices over to a lady who was sitting at the fire. She started examining them.

After a few minutes she said, "They are transmitting signals!"

With this news, cries of joy rang out across the camp. They were going to be saved!

43

WHEW, IT ACTUALLY WORKED!

Everyone started coming over to the children to thank them for what they had done and the risk they had taken to save the Vanished.

"Thank you so much!"

"Blessings upon you!"

"You guys rock!"

Shelshala, Henrite and Kenakada were embarrassed by the attention, but everyone was being so nice they couldn't help but feel really good.

Without raising any alarms, Yokanada and other scientists, who knew there was a chance that the GPS trackers were out of range of a functioning satellite, moved to another fire to talk. If that were the case, it would be a matter of days rather than hours before help arrived, because a complete cosmic search would have to be conducted on Kaka-La.

Only one individual would know the range of the track-ers and Yokanada intended on getting the information from him. He headed over to where Kakamuchu was still sitting alone, sulking by a fire.

As angry as Kakamuchu was, after hearing the kids' story, he could not help admiring what they had accomplished. Never in his wildest dreams would he have thought that Kakalilian kids were capable of high level planning.

"Kakamuchu!" called Yokanada.

Kakamuchu got up from where he was sitting. "What do you want, usurper!" Even when he was clearly defeated, he could not help but be mean. It came naturally.

Yokanada ignored the name-calling. "Are the GPS units in range of a functioning satellite?"

"How should I know? Ask the thieving brats."

"I'm not going to engage with your childish behavior. Are you going to let me know or not?"

"Watch your tone! I am still your Supreme Leader!"

"If you have any decency or compassion in you, a large number of your people have been suffering and finally have hope of being saved. They will be saved either way. I would just like to let them know how long it will take so they won't be disappointed if ships don't show up today!" Yokanada was speaking very calmly, but was feeling very frustrated with Kakamuchu.

"Such crybabies. This is not such a bad place. At least you have food and water. I could have selected somewhere far worse. Besides—"

Kakamuchu's nonsense was interrupted by a group of vanished guards coming up behind him. Even though they did not speak the Kakalilian language very well beyond commands they had been taught, they understood enough to learn that Kakamuchu was on the planet. And, they definitely were not coming over to give him welcome hugs!

144

When he sensed them behind him, Kakamuchu turned around and immediately started hurling abuse at them.

"You bottle-headed ignoramuses! You are all going to pay for this! Once we get back to Kaka-La, I am going to shatter you into a million pieces and throw you into a black hole! You nincompoop wannabes! You are nothing without me! Brains the size of a pea! I made you and this is how you repay me!"

The guards, without their blood pressure stabilizers, all started shooting at Kakamuchu. The deflector he was wearing absorbed the shock of each beam, twisting and turning his body into different shapes.

Yokanada, Shelshala, Henrite, Kenakada and all the other Kakalilians in close range watched the exchange in astonishment. It was so unexpected that it took a few moments for anyone to react. After their initial shock, a few Kakalilians rushed over and stood between Kakamuchu and the guards. The guards stopped shooting as Yokanada addressed them in their language.

"Please calm down!"

The force of all the beams had contorted Kakamuchu's body into the shape of a hexagon, but not even that was preventing him from yelling. The kids could not help but giggle at his funny shape as he continued ranting and raving. As he was slowly returning to his normal form (and still yelling random abuses), a faint humming sound came from afar.

Silence swept across the settlement as everyone turned to one another. Were their minds playing tricks on them?

Was it really a sound? Even Kakamuchu ended his tirade mid-sentence.

After a few moments, it was clear that they were not mistaken; the sound was that of rocket engines! Everyone started talking at the same time.

"It must be ships from Kaka-La!"

"What else could it be?"

"We are saved!"

Excitement and anticipation was in full force when ships became visible on the horizon. One, two, three, four, five... ten ships!

As they landed outside the settlement area, cheers filled the air. And, just as had happened on Laugh-Out-Loud Day on Kaka-La, Shelshala, Henrite and Kenakada were lifted on to shoulders to chants of "Heroes are the best, three of them no less!"

Shelshala, Henrite and Kenakada beamed with joy and relief. Since appearing on this planet, at the back of their minds had been a nagging feeling: what if their plan didn't work? What if they were stuck on this horrible planet like all the other Vanished?

"It worked! It worked! Henrite, you're amazing!" yelled Shelshala to Henrite above the cheers.

"Are you kidding me? This never would have happened without you!" said Henrite.

"Ahem, obviously you both have forgotten that it was all me!" said Kenakada with a smile. "All I can say is I'm glad they showed up now. If I'd had to eat any of those berries, I would have puked!"

All three of the kids started laughing. Kidding aside, they felt amazing.

As the cheers continued, the doors of the landed ships opened and ramps extended to the ground.

44

RESCUED!

The crews on the ships disembarked and joined the celebrations.

Shelshala, Henrite and Kenakada saw their parents getting off one of the ships. They climbed down off the shoulders of the individuals who had been holding them and wheeled at top speed toward them.

Amidst hugs and kisses of relief, Henrite's mom admonished them, "How could you do something so risky? What if he had hurt you? Oh, I don't want to think about it! How did you figure out what to do?"

"I wish I could say we had it planned, Mom," said Henrite. "But, once we were at the palace, it was a combination of on the spot thinking and luck. Shelshala came up with the idea of transferring the deflector to Kakamuchu. Kenakada and I had no idea. We had to kiss his nasty hand." Henrite's sentences tumbled over each other as he made a face of disgust.

"His hand? What? Why?" asked Shelshala's dad.

"Because, my girl knew that was how to get the shield transferred!" said Dr. Kakachala.

Shelshala was uncomfortable with the attention she was getting. "I didn't know, Mom, I sorta guessed. You should have seen Kenakada, though. He threw himself in front of us so the laser wouldn't hit us and then he showed us how to avoid getting hurt by the laser."

All faces turned to Kenakada. He hated the attention even more than Shelshala. "No big deal," he mumbled.

"All I can say is that you were all terrific!" said Kenakada's dad, giving his son another hug.

"Dad, how'd you guys get here so fast?" asked Henrite. "We've only been here about an hour or so."

"It's actually about fourteen hours since you were transported. The transport process probably took around twelve hours or so, but I guess you don't feel the time," said Mr. Kalamayo.

"Oh, that explains it."

Kenakada turned to his parents. "Dad, Mom, Ravro's here! He's fine. I mean sorta fine."

"Let's go find him!" said Kenakada's dad.

Kenakada and his parents headed to the fires where crew members from the ships were distributing nutrition bars and electrolyte enhanced water.

Yokanada stood in the middle of a group, discussing details for evacuation.

Henrite's dad turned to his mom. "Looks like Yokanada is making arrangements with the crew."

"Dad, you know Yokanada?"

"Yes son, he is one of our most gifted astronomers. It was a very sad day when we lost him."

"Boy, you adults are sneaky. I could never tell when you were sad about anything!"

Henrite's mom smiled. "You kids had enough to deal with."

I think it's a good time for Shelshala's dad and me to see if we can be of any assistance. We'll come back and let you know what we learn," said Henrite's dad.

The dads headed over to the group gathered around Yokanada.

Henrite's mom still had her arm wrapped around him and gave him another affectionate squeeze. "You and Shelshala must be very hungry."

"Starving!"

As if someone heard them, long tables piled with food were being wheeled down one of the ships' ramps.

As the first table passed by them, Henrite and Shelshala saw platters of Kakalilian noodles smothered in butter, spaghetti and meatballs, whole roasted turkanos (Kakalilian turkey), fried cluckadoos (Kakalilian chicken), pizazu (Kakalilian pizza), burgohams (Kakalilian hamburgers), Kakalilian fries, stacks and stacks of different kinds of sandwiches: grilled cheese, peanut butter and jelly, turkanos, rosbeeja (Kakalilian roast beef) and picagoja (Kakalilian ham).

As Shelshala and Henrite's stomachs growled with hunger from the sight and smells of the food, a second table passed by them carrying mounds of chocolate bars, cakes of chocolate, vanilla, peanut butter, strawberry and lemon, covered with cream frosting two inches thick, fruit pies, cream pies and bowls filled with different flavors of ice cream.

Their jaws dropped in astonishment.

Shelshala's mom laughed. "Close your mouths before something flies in!"

"How, where..." Henrite tried to ask, but his words came out all jumbled.

"Who made all this?" finished Shelshala.

Tables of food were now coming off all the ships. The aromas were driving the kids mad!

Henrite's mom smiled at their reaction. "Why don't we follow the tables to see where they are going to be set up and Shelshala's mom and I will explain."

They moved toward the settlement.

"When the engineers were finally able to break the code to Kakamuchu's lab—" started Henrite's mom.

"What code?" interrupted Henrite. "There was no code when he took us in."

"As I was going to explain," said his mom with a smile.

"Oops, sorry Mom."

"When a group of engineers and scientists, including Shelshala's parents and your dad, went to the castle to confront Kakamuchu and get the location of the Vanished from him, he wasn't there. They had no idea that you kids had gotten to the castle before them. We assumed you were still celebrating with your friends at school. We should have known better!" she said, tousling Henrite's hair. "I'll let Shelshala's mom explain what happened at the castle."

The tables were being set up in the settlement near the first group of fires. Once the moms confirmed that their help was not needed, they sat down with Shelshala and Henrite at a fire while everything was being arranged.

Shelshala's mom continued. "We knew there was a lab underground at the palace, but could not find the entryway. We assumed Kakamuchu was in the lab and had concealed the entrance. It took about half an hour for the structural engineers to locate it. When you entered the lab, Kakamuchu remotely closed a titanium door behind you that had been designed to seamlessly blend into the wall. The engineers went through millions of number combinations until they identified the code to open it. That took about another half hour. I think, by that time, you guys were no longer in the lab. We only found out that you had been there when we got to the X-Posure and saw the readouts from your scans.

After that, we frantically searched all over the lab for clues to where he might have taken you. I think it was your dad, Henrite, who identified the unusual GPS activity. Once he made the discovery, we deducted that somehow you had all been vanished together. How did that happen with your deflectors?"

"I'm not sure, Mom," said Shelshala. "After we got the deflector on Kakamuchu, he took us into the electromagnetic spectrum chamber. He came in with us and we all had deflectors on, but we still vanished."

"Oh, it sends a chill up my spine just thinking of it," said Henrite's mom. "You children were so brave. But what if he had hurt you! Oh dear, I know it's done. I need to stop thinking about it."

Shelshala's mom held onto Henrite's mom's hand to comfort her and then turned back to Shelshala.

"Most likely he used the X-Posure to identify what materials were in the deflector and adjusted the ray settings."

"Kaladungo Dr. K! I never would have thought!" said Henrite.

"Kakamuchu has always been highly intelligent, since he was a child," said Shelshala's mom. "Unfortunately, he has never used his intelligence in a positive way."

By this time, chairs had been arranged around the tables and Henrite and Shelshala's dads were back. Kenakada, his parents and Ravro were also heading toward them. Ravro looked like a ponggy who was getting a bone for the first time.

"Man, I don't remember the last time I wasn't hungry!" Ravro said as he sat down at the table. "I don't know where to start. This is awesome!"

While the kids had been talking with their parents, nutrition bars and water had been distributed across the settlement and doctors and nurses were treating the ill. It was agreed that the weakest Kakalilians (those who had been on Thereus the longest), children and then adult females were to eat first, with the adult males to follow.

Shelshala, Henrite and Kenakada refused to be among the first group to eat—no matter how much their parents and other Kakalilians insisted.

They each ate a nutrition bar with a drink and stayed right where they were by the fire.

"Where'd all the food come from, Mom?" ask Henrite.

"Once you were located, preparations began for rescue.

Luckily all the cosmic sightseeing ships Kakamuchu had put out of service had not been recycled yet. The astronomers were familiar with the conditions on this planet. As crews were preparing for takeoff, nutrition bars and electrolyte water were being loaded on the ships. At the same time, about a hundred chefs from local restaurants showed up with trucks of food to prepare on the ships. They had learned of the mission through updates on the Crysquid and wanted to provide the Vanished with home cooked hot meals. What a tremendous effort to get everything together in such a short time! They cooked and grubbed the whole way here to make sure there would be enough food for everyone. We are very grateful to them!"

The kids were so happy to see the Vanished feasting and couldn't wait until it was their turn!

45

NO WAY HE'S COMING!

While they were sitting around at the fire waiting for their turn to eat, Henrite wondered how the evacuation was going to work.

"Dad, what's up with the evacuation?"

"As groups finish eating, they will board ships. As soon as a ship is full, it will depart. We are a few ships short for a full evacuation, so some ships will return for a second flight. At that time, the guards will be taken back to their planet and Kakamuchu will be brought back to Kaka-La.

When the children heard that Kakamuchu would return to Kaka-La, the boys were furious.

"Dad, that's not fair!" exclaimed Henrite in disbelief.

"He's the reason everyone was stuck here!" added Kenakada. "He's bad news. We should leave him here to rot!"

"Boys," said Henrite's dad, "we will follow the code of conduct we have been taught, especially when our emotions make our judgment hazy."

"What's right about taking him back to Kaka-La?" asked Henrite.

"He will have his day in court and the Kakalilians will decide his fate. That is what is right."

"I hope they decide to pulverize him!" said Henrite.

His mom had been listening to the exchange and jokingly said to her husband, "Sounds like we might need to get some anti-aggression serum ready when we get home!" Then turning to the boys she said, "Remember, disregard for others created this tragedy. Compassion will put an end to it."

"Come on guys, we beat him!" said Shelshala. "Everyone gets to go home and no more stupid decrees! Who cares what happens to him now!"

After all they had gone through because of Kakamuchu, Henrite and Kenakada were definitely not feeling very generous, no matter what their parents said.

"Yes, that's all really great. But, I still hope they decide to blow him to smithereens!" said Henrite.

Kenakada gave Henrite a nudge with his elbow. "Dude, I got a dose of that anti-aggression stuff when I was a kid. We already had to kiss his ugly hand. Trust me, you don't want to fight the urge to hug him all day!"

Everyone laughed at Kenakada's warning.

When the first group had finished eating, the kids' parents insisted that they must eat next. It didn't take much persuasion! The tables had been reset and all the dishes replenished. Everything looked so good, they didn't know where to begin. Once they did start eating, they wolfed down so much food, they could barely get up from the table.

"Yikes, I don't feel so good," said Henrite, pushing back his chair after finishing off his meal with one scoop of each of the fifteen flavors of ice cream.

"Did you have to eat all that ice cream? Of course you don't feel good. You'll be lucky if you don't throw up!" said Shelshala.

"Aagh, don't say throw up! I'm seriously unwell!" Henrite did look a little yellow. "Mom! I feel sick!"

"Oh Henrite! Come over here," his mom called out from the fire the parents were sitting at. "The medical team brought a stomach settling tonic in case the Vanished had trouble digesting food after not eating for so long. It wasn't meant for YOU, but I'll get some."

"Thanks Mom," moaned Henrite.

Shelshala and Kenakada could not help but laugh, as he stumbled away from the table with his hands crossed over his stomach.

By the time Henrite had taken some tonic and rested a bit, it was their turn to board one of the ships heading home. Once they were settled in their cabin with their moms, the kids almost fell asleep where they were standing.

Next thing they knew, their moms were waking them and giving them piggyback rides home.

46

A SECOND CHANCE

Celebrations continued for weeks. Schools were closed, work hours were cut, candy factories re-opened and market hours extended. Every day was a party!

The Kakalilians voted to no longer have a Supreme Leader. Instead, each neighborhood would select a representative and all the representatives would work together to share Kaka-La's riches with all Kakalilians. The castle and its extensive laboratory were opened to everyone.

Shelshala and Henrite's team won the *Kaka-La* Speed Relay Race. Kenakada cheered them on from the front row. It was really amazing all the things they had accomplished using science. The thermodynamic principles and physics that they used to super charge their turbochargers had worked like a charm. Henrite had a little accident and scraped up his arm against a wall. But that was totally his own fault: he lost his concentration when Pamalali Kanakalala, one of the cutest girls in their class, winked at him as she passed him on a curve.

As for Kakamuchu, after Kakalilians learned about his childhood of all studying without any kind of affection, laughter, or fun, they felt he deserved a second chance at a life full of fun, friends and learning. It was agreed he would be given the anti-memory serum Ouch-Out, which was used in very small doses when children had bad accidents learning how to wheel. The serum erased two to five minutes of memory at the normal dosage level. Doctors multiplied the dose to a level that would make Kakamuchu forget everything in his life back to when he was three years old.

So if, by chance, space travel takes you to another galaxy and you happen to visit Kaka-La, look for Kakamuchu. He is in preschool, laughing and playing with all the kids and going to his two new homes where he plays slimeball with his new families, the Kakachalas and the Kalamayos, eats lots of candy and gets big hugs—just because.

THE END

Made in the USA
Las Vegas, NV
17 June 2022